SNOW IS FALLING, COCOA IS CALLING!

THE COFFEE LOFT FALL SEASON SERIES

KIMBERLEY MONTPETIT

SNOW IS FALLING, COCOA IS CALLING!

SNOW IS FALLING, COCOA IS CALLING!

MANSION WEDDING

SECRET IDENTITY

SNOW IS FALLING, COCOA IS CALLING!

LEFT AT THE ALTAR

STUCK TOGETHER BLIZZARD

KIMBERLEY MONTPETIT

WEDDING PLANNER

CHAPTER 1

CAITEY

*C*aitey Belgrave stomped on the brakes of her SUV, peering through the windshield at a dark forest thick with towering trees that blinded her to everything else in the vicinity.

The abrupt braking caused the wedding items piled on every surface in the rear storage area of her SUV, including the back seat and the passenger seat next to her, to shift and slide while she cringed in terror at potential breakage.

Thank goodness nothing fell to the floor. Wedding paraphernalia was coming out of her eyeballs!

Even so, Caitey threw out a hand to prevent potential breakage of the bride & groom crystal goblets, specially ordered by her cousin, Jenna Thornton—AKA "the bride." Jenna had sent Caitey darn good money for the gorgeous things, and she'd had them specially engraved with Jenna's and her fiancé Logan's names in beautiful gold letters.

The winding road was dense with foliage. Sky-high redwoods, pine trees, and giant oaks towered overhead as she climbed higher into the California mountain on a paved but incredibly narrow and winding road. After several hairpin turns, Caitey's stomach was roiling.

Taking the last sip from her water bottle, Caitey was tempted to pull over to the side of the road to get some fresh air after the nearly four-hour drive from San Diego.

Wasn't she nearly there? So far—after thirty minutes of slow driving up the mountain road from the highway exit— she'd passed estate after estate every quarter mile or so; gorgeous homes with multiple acres of forest, manicured lawns, and flower gardens.

There was money up here—lots of it.

Jenna hadn't told her that she was about to marry a millionaire!

Address numbers disappeared a mile behind Caitey. How would she find the right place? Pausing on the empty road, she consulted her phone map again.

She startled when a British-accented AI woman's voice suddenly announced: "You have arrived."

"Oh, yeah?" Caitey muttered, gazing at nothing but dense trees and a road that curved endlessly, going nowhere. "Brilliant."

Taking her foot off the brake, the vehicle slowly inched

forward—and that's when she spied an address marker about two hundred yards further on.

Well, maybe not. No numbers. No street name, even. Or maybe she missed it due to too much nature!

All at once, she spied a massive and spectacular ironwork of arched front gates to the next estate. She stopped again, putting the car in Park so she could lean across the passenger seat to see through the window more easily.

Pressing the button to roll down her window, Caitey gulped at the impressive entrance. "This *is* it," she whispered aloud.

The name of the mansion house was crafted into the ironwork of the front gates in fancy letters.

HEARST WOODS ESTATE

All at once, she felt tiny and insignificant. She glanced at the contents of her loaded car, the packed trunk, and backseat crammed with wedding stuff, and knew it wasn't enough for a site as large as this mansion.

What was Jenna thinking of hiring a still-new, small wedding planner for an estate of this magnitude? Caitey hoped her cousin wouldn't hate her later if she couldn't properly pull it off.

Especially after the debacle of her first job at the prestigious interior decorating company. She'd received an excellent salary straight out of college but found herself working double shifts with expectations that changed daily.

And her boss, a dragon lady named Darla Wolff—who gave her little training—yelled all day long. Even when small, easily fixed things didn't go precisely as *Darla* would have done.

After all, Caitey wasn't a mind-reader! Eventually, she found herself dreading going to work every day. A few years later, she was unceremoniously fired in front of the entire staff, on purpose to humiliate her. Ms. Wolff told Caitey that she would never work in the industry again. No recommendations, no referrals, no references.

Months went by while Caitey pounded the pavement for another job until the day Jenna called her up and begged her to create her wedding at a country estate. At the time, she didn't realize it was one of the biggest family names in California—the powerhouse Hearst family!

Talk about stress! Of course, Caitey said yes—since her bank account was down to zero—and the plans began!

Now that it was here, she couldn't help but second-guess her expertise and ability to do right by her sweet cousin. Caitey took a sip from her water bottle, stuck her Nissan SUV in Park and exited, walking apprehensively toward the massive double gates. How did she get inside? No one appeared to be on the premises. She couldn't even catch a glimpse of any actual house through the forest of trees.

Then she saw the keypad and remembered that Jenna had given her a code to use since she would be the first to arrive.

Pulling out her phone, she found the gate code and entered it.

Slowly, the double gates began to open. "Yikes!" she cried, returning to her vehicle and jumping into the driver's seat. Hurriedly, she backed up so the thousand-pound gate wouldn't pick up her car and push it across the road and over the cliff.

A niggle of excitement shot up her throat as she entered, tires crunching on the gravel, at the sight of the oversized gate closing shut in her rearview mirror.

She prayed she could pull this wedding off. Her cousin said they would all pitch in and help, but the wedding party would be much too busy, and guests were, well, *guests*! At least there was still a full day—tomorrow—before the first guests arrived.

Caitey rolled down the side window and a cool cross breeze wafted across her cheeks. The temperature had lowered dramatically from the freeway. She had to be two or three thousand feet higher than the Pacific Ocean coastline.

Overhead, the dense trees rattled their leaves while Caitey leaned forward to peer through the windshield at the twisted limbs of old oaks and a carpet of pine needles and grasses that muted any sound. Nerves knocked at her throat, nibbling away at her confidence.

This was *not* typical Southern California weather in the fall, which was usually mild. But she was in the mountains now. Summer was a far distant memory, and Autumn was fast disappearing, too.

Slowly, Caitey drove down the narrow, paved entrance, her palms sweating, and her heart pounding as her vehicle crept through wild bushes with sunlight dripping through the dense trees.

This was exactly how she pictured Manderley Estate on the coast of England! That iconic and mysterious house on the cliffs of Cornwall overlooking the ocean from her favorite novel, *Rebecca,* by Daphne du Maurier.

Last night, I dreamt I went to Manderley . . . except it was today, more than a decade after she read that book as a teen.

But she was driving in a cool-ish California afternoon in early November. There was no idyllic British countryside or ocean waves pounding in the distance.

Might there be a romantic pond or lake somewhere on the property? A potential location for the wedding reception?

At the moment, the only thing before Caitey's eyes were overgrown trees, brambly bushes, and half a mile of deep woods. She wondered if she had taken a wrong turn since there was no sign of a yard or house in the distance—even though she was on the only road after pulling through the gate.

Finally, the pavement widened, and the ominous woods faded, revealing a splendid stone manor house with chimneys and balconies and a circular drive. Ivy crawled up the stone walls, and the expanse of upper story windows shone in the afternoon sunshine, sparkling off the glass.

The riot of wildflowers along the drive became a breathtaking rose garden with flowers of every color. Caitey gasped at its beauty.

She slowed her SUV in front of the steps to the massive double front doors. "Okay, *cousin*. You said it was a nice house, not practically a castle."

Caitey bit her lips, throat dry. Her usually composed and unruffled wedding planner persona shrank just a bit in her seat.

"I think I need a second pair of hands to pull this off," she muttered to herself.

Turning off the engine, Caitey unfolded herself from the seat. She was overdressed for the task of unloading all the wedding paraphernalia she'd stowed. She had assumed there might be family or staff that could help her.

Not a soul in sight. No greeting, no other parked vehicles. Where was everybody?

Had she driven up on the wrong day?

Her stomach growled. She'd forgotten to eat lunch; by now, it was mid-afternoon.

Digging into her handbag, Caitey found a granola bar, peeled it open to take a bite, then gulped down the last of her water.

The grounds were both wild and lovely. Burgeoning flower beds and an exquisite rose garden. She'd have to tour the entire property for that hoped-for fountain.

Brushing crumbs from her palms along the sides of her sheath dress, she turned in a circle, gazing at the woods and the grounds before stepping onto the stone path, then the wide steps to the front door, and rang the bell.

A beautiful melodic chime echoed through the house, but

7

nobody answered. Not a sound anywhere. No passing traffic —although she wouldn't hear any vehicles this far into the private property.

Perhaps everyone was in the back of the house unloading chairs and tables.

A prickle ran up her neck. Feeling like the only person in the world right now was eerie. And then a new thought bounced around her brain.

What if she had the wrong house? She hadn't seen a number. There was no mailbox, just her Google map telling her she had arrived. But the code Jenna had given her opened the property gate, so she *was* in the right place.

Whirling on the ball of her foot, Caitey decided the only thing to do was drive around to the back of the house and find any sign of life—or people.

A dark shadow flitted in the woods when she lifted her eyes. Her heart clutched with anxiety, and Caitey swallowed hard. It must be one of the grounds men—or maybe just a squirrel.

The shadow moved again, but it was not a bird or a squirrel. The shadow was human.

"Yoohoo, it's the wedding planner here!" she called out, her voice snatched away by the open expanse of the property. "Anyone around?"

Silence, except for a breeze rustling the oaks and pines.

Impatiently, she tripped down the stone steps, climbed into her vehicle, and inserted the key into the Nissan's ignition, bringing the engine back to life.

That shadowy figure moved closer to the circular drive when she put the car into gear to drive around to the back.

It was a man in a black suit, crisp white shirt, and tie, watching her from inside the forest, a shadow of darkness against the thicket of trees. A pair of binoculars dangling from his hands.

Caitey's heart jumped into her throat, a gasp of fear freezing her into place. But the man stayed in the shadows, not coming forward to greet her.

He must be a groundskeeper—but since when did gardeners wear three-thousand-dollar Armani suits?

CHAPTER 2

CAITEY

Slowing the car, Caitey rolled down her side window. "Is anybody there?" she called again, but her voice was now hoarse and timid.

Caitey blinked. Wait a minute! The man in the Armani suit wasn't there any longer. He was . . . gone, just like that.

Had she dreamed him up? Or had he disappeared because he was an apparition?

She blew out a long, shaky breath. Was she losing her mind? Stress-induced apparitions reminiscent of all the past spooky books and movies she'd enjoyed over the years?

Yes, Caitey had to admit that she was easily influenced. Hiding under the bed covers and reading mysteries was her favorite thing, but afterward, she had to sleep with the light on!

Her mother would find her huddled underneath the blankets and then throw them off to make a game out of seeing her there—as if she was still four years old and they were playing hide-and-seek.

"Whew, Caitey," she would exclaim as if she'd been searching for hours. "It's a good thing I found you. Otherwise, this nice cup of hot cocoa would go to waste." Then she'd give her a wink. "Or I'd have to drink it myself."

A smile crept over her lips, remembering those nights so long ago when Dad was traveling out of town for his government work.

"Oh, look," Mom would suddenly announce, "I have a cocoa for you, and a second cup for me!"

Then she'd perch on the edge of the bed while they drank their cocoa like proper ladies, sticking their pinky finger out and speaking in a British accent while they discussed books or movies for hours.

Whenever she had a stressful wedding, Caitey desperately wished her mother was here helping her. Mom was Mrs. Organizer Specialist herself. Her personality and talent came in handy when the embassy in Portugal—where her parents had been living the past five years—had to plan a dinner, a gala, or special meetings with heads of state.

"I desperately need to hire an assistant," Caitey muttered, glancing in her rearview mirror as she drove around the circular drive to the mansion's rear.

Laughter gurgled in her throat. Like she could afford an assistant—not. But her parents would arrive tomorrow, flying in from Lisbon to attend Jenna's wedding.

She couldn't wait to see them—and have an extra pair of hands! She knew Dad would spend all his time with his brother-in-law, Uncle Alexander Thornton, Jenna's father.

Caitey peered through the windshield as she turned the corner. The house was just as beautiful here as the magnificent front entrance.

There were more flower gardens, towering trees, and what looked like an orchard far beyond the manicured lawns and stone pathways.

Plumes of water sprayed from a fountain, sparkling in the sunlight. It was breathtaking and a perfect location for her cousin's special day.

Despite being early November, the sun shone, and the reception would be lovely in this idyllic setting after the indoor ceremony.

Unless Jenna changed her mind.

Brides did that. A lot. They changed their minds about nearly everything.

At least Caitey wasn't doing the actual catering, prepping the food or decorating the cake. During their planning sessions over the phone the last few months, Jenna had decided it was easier to hire those jobs out. *Caitey* was merely the wedding planner, the decorator, and the one keeping the schedule—making sure everything happened on time and solving any problems.

Or meltdowns, as the case may be.

At least this wedding was smaller and more intimate than most.

Just last week, Jenna had breathed a happy sigh on the phone: "I'm so glad you're doing my wedding. I won't have to worry about a thing because I know you will make it all *perfect!*"

At the time, Caitey could only smile wanly. She hoped she could pull it off, but none of the weddings she had done over the past seven years had lived up to that tall order. Something always went wrong, even if it was something small. A wedding planner could count on it!

Weddings had too many details and variables and personalities to make happy. But she prided herself on coming pretty darn close. So far, since she'd started her own bridal business, Caitey's online reviews averaged 4.5 out of 5 stars.

Caitey rolled to a stop in the gravel parking lot behind the mansion, her eyes flitting in every direction. The back of the estate was just as quiet as the front, and it appeared there was official parking on the far side of the gardens.

But hers was the only vehicle.

Where was everybody?

When she turned off the engine and slid out of her seatbelt, Caitey lifted a hand against the sun's glare. The property extended as far as she could see.

Deeper into the private woods, she spied a narrow lane that led to a garage that looked as if it could hold ten vehicles.

Another sign of the Hearst wealth.

About two hundred miles north of Los Angeles she'd

toured the infamous Hearst Castle during her college years for a weekend getaway with roommates to drool over the rich and famous from the 1920s. The house—more like a castle with multiple swimming pools, gorgeous architecture and gardens oozed money from every corner.

Caitey had concluded that William Randolph Hearst was richer than the queen of England.

When she stepped out of the car, Caitey's high heels crunched on the fine gravel and her ankles wobbled a tiny bit. Maybe she should have worn sneakers, but she didn't want to arrive in jeans if she met Jenna's fiancé and his family in the first five minutes.

Furtively, she glanced about to ensure she was alone, and then Caitey laughed at her silliness. The dude in the woods had spooked her, but he was probably just an early-arriving family member taking a walk through the trees.

Even so, who wore a suit to go walking in the woods? The wedding wasn't for two days. And why wouldn't the strange man at least raise a hand in greeting to acknowledge her?

The perimeter of the mansion was empty of any people or activity. Quiet, undisturbed, as if the estate's residents no longer existed.

She had sent a quick text to Jenna while driving through the village at the foot of the mountains before starting up the winding road that led to this neighborhood of mansions and sprawling estates nestled within the mountain forest.

That was at least thirty minutes ago, and she still hadn't received a response back.

She had expected to see Jenna throw open the back doors and run full speed toward her as soon as she parked.

But all was silent as a tomb.

How about a gardener? A housekeeper? A chauffeur waxing the Rolls Royce?

Caitey gave a small laugh. None in sight.

"Guess I'll let myself in," she murmured, striding up the stone path that wound past an English country garden of hollyhocks, daisies, lavender, peonies, irises, and golden California poppies.

A balance of traditional elegance and romantic whimsy.

A tickle of awe and envy rose up her chest even as she smiled at the exquisite beauty. "I could live out here forever."

All she needed was a book, a chair under the shade of one of those massive oak trees, and a cold lemonade. A life of perfect leisure.

At each turn of the paths stood tall Roman goddess statues wearing alabaster dresses, guarding magnificent water fountains and manicured hedges. Caitey spotted her reflection in the shallow water.

The scent of flowers was like a perfume factory. Sweet and heady.

At the rear double oak doors, Caitey knocked timidly, then rang the bell. But all she could hear was the echo of the chime reverberating inside an empty house.

Boldly, she yanked the doorknob and pulled. Locked up tight.

All at once, her phone buzzed, and Caitey gave a start. It was a text from Jenna. At last!

Are you at the house yet?

Caitey quickly punched at her phone. **Yes. Where *are* you??**

Jenna sent an upside-down smile. **We got stuck in the village at the base of the mountain. A flat tire. Had to be towed to the mechanic. I'm so sorry! The parents are all away from the house, too, but Marcus could let you in. Your bedroom is upstairs on the left, second door down. A full ensuite. Make yourself at home! See you soon!**

Caitey sent a sad emoji. **Wow, I'm so sorry. What a bummer when you're running around doing last-minute wedding stuff. P.S. Who is Marcus? There's no one here but me!**

Well, if she didn't count the spooky dude hiding in the woods.

She waited a minute, staring at her phone, but there was no response.

She plopped onto one of the wrought-iron benches and tried not to be annoyed. The sun was hot on her head, and her water bottle was long emptied. The front and back mansion doors were locked . . . except she hadn't looked for a side door.

Ten minutes later, after checking every side door, garage door, and first-floor window, Caitey was ready to scream when Jenna finally texted back. Hopefully, they were almost here! Unfortunately, she had started hoping too soon.

I'm so sorry, honey. We're still waiting for the car to get fixed, and we're about a twenty-minute drive from you. At least, we're in the village you passed on the way up the mountain and not Santa Barbara! So, it'll be about an hour until

The message stopped as if Jenna had disappeared. Caitey groaned. "What?!"

Then suddenly, Jenna continued.

On second thought, get back in your car and drive down to our little mountain village. There's a Coffee Loft shop on Main that recently opened. Get yourself a cold drink, a frothy latte, or hot chocolate with those giant marshmallows, and tell them you're my cousin! Tata!

Immediately, Caitey dialed her cousin's number so she could speak in person, but it went straight to voicemail. What the heck!

Annoyed, she growled in her throat, listening to the birds singing in the pine trees. There was no sign of the lurking guy, thank goodness, but she still stared in every direction. It was freaky being alone while a man lurked in the shadows of the woods.

Despite the lovely gardens perfumed by roses and lavender, Caitey did not plan to sit here by herself for five minutes, let alone an hour or two.

CHAPTER 3

MARCUS

*M*arcus Stirling checked the security cameras around the Hearst property, one by one, to ensure they were all working properly.

He loved being back at this family estate and in the dense woods, working at what he did best—surveillance.

So far, two cameras had stopped recording, and three others needed new batteries. Once he'd replaced the batteries and fastened two new cameras at strategic locations, he headed for the house to check the rest.

His best friend Logan, who was like a brother, was getting married in two days, and since Logan was high profile with a historically wealthy family as part of the Hearst legend, security was of the utmost importance.

Marcus was intrigued to meet Logan's fiancée, too. Jenna was from New Orleans, which was interesting. Logan met

Jenna Thornton two years earlier when he traveled there to meet investors in a new venture.

Logan told Marcus that on a whim, he had stopped at one of the Coffee Loft shops for a drink, and he and Jenna had instantly hit it off. By the time he had spent an hour drinking his double espresso to keep him awake for an evening meeting, they were joking and laughing like long-time friends.

Logan asked her out the next night for dinner.

Marcus wished it was that easy for *him* to meet new women. Despite trying, he hadn't had a date in a year, but the women he met in the Santa Barbara or Los Angeles areas were too rich and spoiled for his tastes.

They were either wanna-be actresses who would do anything for a part in a commercial or movie, or they came from money and only talked about shopping or people in the Hollywood world they knew—or D.C. politicians.

His distaste for both made him incompatible with every woman he met at a party or event.

In contrast, although considered part of the nouveau riche, Logan's parents had bought this secluded piece of property because of its beautiful oak, pine, and walnut trees. The old British surname of Hearst meant "woods or forest," after all.

Of course, his best friend's family was nothing like European royalty. William Randolph Hearst had become *American royalty,* like the Vanderbilts and the Astors, although he was a generation later than the original railroad tycoons of the late 19th century.

Although Marcus didn't come from the same world as Logan, they'd been friends since childhood, running wild on the property, building forts, making guns out of sticks, yelling like a commando during a battle. Their bond strengthened as they played football in high school and even took a few college classes together.

But after college graduation, he struck out on his own, joining the Navy and training to be a SEAL. Ten years later, he retired and started his own security firm, which he loved.

He had a nose for suspicious people or events and was like a hound dog, following the scent.

Despite being able to shimmy up an electric pole to install cameras and listening devices, he wore a suit when he was part of a big event—like meetings and weddings.

Today, there was no tree climbing going on. He had to be professional and in his best suit when guests arrived. And back to being just Logan's best friend. Not the hired security.

Marcus lifted his head after he checked the final camera and synchronized it with the receiver inside the house.

Seconds later, he halted in his tracks. His phone was notifying him of movement at the front gate. Marcus quickly pulled up the feed for the camera in that location.

A suspicious vehicle—a Nissan SUV—had stopped before the double wrought-iron gates. The car crept forward, slowed again, and then stopped.

Suddenly a young woman shoved the driver door open and climbed out.

She was loitering much too long, and the hair on

Marcus's neck prickled. This one needed deeper investigation.

The woman glanced about, spinning on her high heels while looking back over her shoulder and down the road several times. Hm. Apparently, she was lost.

Consulting her phone, she tapped on it. Probably checking Google Maps.

Rechecking the road for oncoming traffic, she frowned, then stared pointedly at the double gates of the Hearst Estate.

Walking forward, she appeared to find the keypad and proceeded to enter a few numbers.

The gates began to open slowly, squeaking in the quiet afternoon silence. Marcus made a mental note to oil them. This woman obviously had the correct code, but nobody had told Marcus there was an arrival this afternoon.

She must be part of the wedding party. But Logan and Jenna's wedding was still two days away. Maybe she was delivering wedding trappings or paraphernalia.

Perhaps a salesclerk with Jenna's wedding gown? A wedding gift by special delivery? Normally, those came by courier, if not FedEx delivery.

Marcus silently watched her car maneuver the winding roads through the woods. He sprinted at times to keep up with her, his feet not making a sound on the soft dirt. Skirting the tree trunks, he remained out of sight while she passed.

She pulled around the circular drive and stopped.

A moment or two later, the woman stepped out of her car and shaded her eyes from the afternoon sun.

Marcus knew there was no one at home, but this woman didn't know that.

He stopped behind a tree and continued to watch. Now that he was closer to the driveway, he pulled out a small pair of binoculars and adjusted the lens.

Her car was loaded with stuff.

She had the longest, silkiest mahogany brown hair he'd ever seen. It swayed in the mild afternoon breeze. She wore a dress and heels and carried a large handbag.

Was she a friend of Jenna's? Since Jenna was in town that afternoon with Logan, Marcus assumed this woman had arrived unannounced.

Which meant he needed to keep an eye on her.

An unannounced guest not on the daily "list" was a person of interest. To watch, study, and intercept if necessary.

Slowly, Marcus moved forward, staying behind the trees but never taking his eyes off her.

The woman quirked her chin to the left—toward him—and her facial features came into view. He was startled to see how perfectly *interesting* she was: a perfect, straight nose, a generous mouth with ruby-red lips, and wispy bangs that drifted across startling cornflower blue eyes.

These new binoculars were terrific, with up-close and personal details.

Marcus sucked in a breath. She was absolutely beautiful. Not in a flashy "look, I'm a model" way, but with a natural, fresh beauty he normally didn't see in Southern California, where women dressed to the nines and wore an inch of makeup, especially in Beverly Hills or downtown Santa Barbara.

Marcus let out a breath that turned into a low whistle. This woman had great legs and an hourglass figure. A tingling sensation ran down his neck, spreading throughout his limbs.

The young woman slowly turned in a circle to take in the estate, holding a hand over her eyes from the sun's glare while she called out—twice.

She bit at those remarkable lips of hers and suddenly froze.

Marcus froze, too.

Without thinking, he'd stepped out from behind the tree where he'd been hiding. He was in full view of her now. He'd foolishly dropped his incognito self.

She gave a start, staggering backward while staring daggers at him.

He stared back, his limbs melting.

Hopefully, she couldn't determine what he was doing in the woods.

From the expression on her face, he'd freaked her out. Hurriedly, she climbed into her vehicle and drove to the back of the house.

He'd not just startled her, he'd frightened her. He was a

stranger, after all. Lurking in the woods while the entire Hearst family was in the village running errands.

Unfortunately, he'd updated the cameras on the estate too late. Logan had asked him a week ago since he wanted no trouble during the week of his wedding, and Marcus had only just now completed the task.

There had been prowlers on the video feed the previous month. The images appeared to be kids. He had yet to figure out how they got over a 12-foot wall or the gate. That was his next step. Find any breaches in the wall perimeter or any loose boards in the rear fence line behind the garages.

In the videos, the boys darted behind trees and climbed some of the older ones with low-hanging limbs. Perhaps they were playing hide-and-seek.

The Hearst Woods *were* the perfect spot. He and Logan had spent a lot of time enjoying adventures in their child-hood days and even into their teens.

The rear grounds of the estate were just as good. The perfect place to get lost—mentally *and* hide out from the parents—until dinner time when their stomachs were growling so loud, they were convinced they would starve to death.

Logan would hold his stomach and moan, "I'm *starving.*"

"No, *I'm* starving!" Marcus would challenge. "What's for dinner? Is Gus cooking tonight?"

"The grownups are having quiche Lorraine, red wine, and a healthy salad. That's an exact quote from Gus to my mother."

"Yuck, do we have to eat the salad, too?" Marcus groaned.

"*We're* having hamburgers. Chips and sodas. At least, that was the order I put in for us. We'll see if Mum gives in." Then a sly grin would cross Logan's face "She usually does when you're visiting. Mum likes you."

"She has to like me. I'm like her adopted son."

Of course, that wasn't true. Even though there was no relation, it often felt like they were brothers, and Marcus was at home here, as if he belonged.

Being careful not to be seen again, Marcus skirted the circular drive and moved carefully down the perimeter wall.

He'd been having an internal debate about whether he should approach the beautiful woman and talk to her, but finally decided to stay put so he didn't blow his cover of being security as well as a guest.

Oops. There she was again. Out of the car, trying the back doorbell, but Marcus knew nobody was home at the moment. Even if Gus was on site, he never answered the door while prepping dinner.

Where *was* Logan and his fiancée, Jenna? They had been gone a long time. Obviously, they were expecting this new woman today. Her Nissan was practically leaking wedding stuff.

Now she was on her phone, talking to someone. Most likely Jenna, he deduced.

Pressing her lips together in frustration, the woman jumped up from the garden bench where she had been sitting for a few minutes and jumped into her car again, peeling around the property heading back up the long drive to the front gates on the paved mountain road.

Marcus could see her on the cameras.

Once she got to the top of the road, the woman pressed the buttons on the keypad, and the gates opened.

After driving through, her SUV disappeared back *down* the mountainside. Toward the village. Because that was the only thing at the edge of this forest.

CHAPTER 4

CAITEY

Caitey's tires spit gravel as she peeled out of the Hearst Estate. She flew down the winding mountain road, then slowed in case another vehicle came around one of the sharp curves.

She wasn't upset at Jenna. Or anyone, really. She was just tired after driving so many hours up from San Diego, especially during rush hour and bumper-to-bumper traffic.

Her right calf was aching from all the starts and stops—at least a hundred times. Then, there was the accident on Highway 5 and horrendous traffic through the Los Angeles area.

She was hungry because she hadn't eaten any lunch, her water was long gone, and she'd hoped to be safely ensconced in her guest suite with all the wedding paraphernalia unpacked by now.

But Caitey *had* spotted the Coffee Loft shop Jenna mentioned on the phone when she drove through town. Thankfully her drive back to the village was passing quickly and she was almost there.

Coffee or tea wasn't her thing, but she assumed they had cold drinks—and hopefully snacks—or she'd fall over and faint from hunger! A giant donut sounded perfect right about now.

Jenna hadn't told her exactly where the Coffee Loft was located, but the village at the bottom of the mountain only had one Main Street, so it wasn't like Caitey would get lost trying to find it. Only if she had a bad sense of direction would she possibly miss finding something she'd already gone past not too long ago, in a small town.

A few minutes later, she spotted the cute shop and pulled into a parking space, letting out a sigh of relief.

She took a moment to catch her breath and sent a text to Jenna to let her know she was at the Coffee Loft in case her friend arrived at the Hearst home, and she wasn't there.

Then she sent a text to her parents. **I made it to Hearst Estate. It's spectacular and intimidating, but a gorgeous spot for the wedding. I can't wait to see you both tomorrow night!**

Caitey finally climbed out of her car, careful to lock her doors, and hoped nobody would break in and steal any wedding decorations.

While walking through the door of the coffee shop, she winced at the ache in her toes. She'd never been able to walk all day in heels, so it was a good thing she was basically self-employed so she could determine her work attire.

The warm, rich scent of freshly brewed coffee filled the air, mixed with the sweet smell of yeasty pastries and a hint of cinnamon, chocolate, and cream from the kitchen.

"May I help you, ma'am?" a young woman said at the counter.

Caitey winced. Did she look like a ma'am? She had just turned twenty-nine, but still. Of course, the counter girl looked no more than twenty.

She studied the menu and then ordered a large Dr Pepper with extra ice and a cinnamon bagel with walnut honey cream cheese. She loved the Coffee Loft's hot cocoa, but she was hot and tired and needed some caffeine!

Behind her, the line grew. The shop bell over the door chimed repeatedly behind her, but in less than a minute after ringing up Caitey's credit card, the girl handed over her order.

She shoved the card into the side pocket of her handbag and pivoted on her heel to scan the shop for a booth.

A tall, husky man was right behind her in line. She hadn't noticed that he was so close. When she turned, Caitey practically launched her order right into his chest. Her drink sloshed and a moment of panic rose up her throat when she almost tossed the entire soda on his suit coat.

Suit coat.

Caitey's eyes darted from his chest all the way up to his

face, gripping her food while her handbag slid off her shoulder.

The man behind her had shoulders like an offensive tackle in the Superbowl. His jaw was chiseled, those lips were full and dreamy, topped by deep chocolate eyes and thick dark brown hair in the perfect short and sleek masculine haircut.

His expression was one of interest, but a touch of amusement sparkled in his eyes as if enjoying her shock while she tried to hang on to her drink.

A shiver ran down Caitey's body at their close proximity. Then she narrowed her eyes. "*You,*" she said in a hoarse whisper. "You're that *guy*! That guy in the woods . . . right? Am I right?"

He blinked at her as if she was speaking Martian.

She stepped backward, nerves on high alert, palms turning sweaty. "Are you some kind of stalker?"

Caitey was tempted to throw her bagel and drink into his face, but the man quickly stepped backward as if sensing danger, holding up his hands.

"Whoa, there. I'm just a customer like you."

When Caitey called him a stalker, the rest of the line whipped their heads toward them. One woman took a quick step back, distancing herself. The other customers just seemed grumpy at the delay.

A man said, "Move out of the line, please!"

Embarrassed, Caitey clutched at her order and stepped

aside, her face burning. The room blurred and then cleared as she spotted an empty table by the picture windows.

She walked toward it, head down, doing her best to ignore the rest of the room. Thankfully, it wasn't *too* busy. Mid-afternoon was in between the lunch and dinner rush. Setting down her drink and bagel plate, she sank into the chair and put a hand to her hot face.

Her body stayed rigid. Caitey desperately wanted to glance behind her, but she did not want to let *that guy* know she was looking at him.

Setting her handbag on the empty chair next to her, she blew out her breath and took a big drink. The burn of cold Dr Pepper was a rush of sanity and slowed down her pounding heart.

Opening the two sides of her bagel, she spread the cream cheese on it and took a tiny bite.

She sensed a shadow moving in close and jerked her head up mid-chew.

It was him again. She had hoped he'd get his order and leave. Caitey couldn't get rid of the image burned into her eyes of that man staring at her from the shadows of the woods.

Talk about freak-out!

"May I sit down?" his low masculine voice asked.

Caitey gulped and almost choked on the bite of bagel. "*No!*" she blurted out on instinct.

His features and voice softened. "I'm terribly sorry I startled you back at the house. I didn't mean to. I'm *not* a stalker. At all."

He paused, gazing at her, his eyes roving her face appreciatively. It had been a long time since Caitey had been looked at in that manner. It was disconcerting but also nice to be admired.

His chocolate brown eyes latched on to hers and held them for a tiny moment. His lips turned into a smile with perfect white teeth, and suddenly this guy looked like a Boy Scout. Impish, friendly, puzzled, and apologetic.

"May I explain?" he asked, gesturing to the empty seat across the table from Caitey.

"Um, I guess so," she finally murmured. "It *is* a public place. I don't intend to make *another* scene."

He slid into the chair opposite her. "Neither do I. By the way, I'm Marcus Hearst—well, actually, Stirling. I mentioned Hearst so you'd know who I'm connected to."

Caitey sat up straighter. "Hearst? You're related to the Hearst family that owns the estate? You *are* the guy I saw. What were you doing lurking in the woods?"

"I wasn't lurking, just doing reconnaissance."

"Huh? *Reconnaissance?* Is there going to be a skirmish?" she quipped. "How are you connected to them?"

"Logan Hearst is my best friend. I take care of the cameras and video for the estate's security, especially when there is a big event, party, or meeting. Or family reunion. Which doesn't happen that often. Mostly weddings and funerals are when family gets together, right?"

A smile crept over Caitey's lips. That was funny. She blew out her breath. "You were installing cameras," she stated.

He nodded. "Putting in new ones, checking the old ones. Not just the woods, but the rear grounds and the house, too."

"But it's a gated estate with a keypad for security. Does it require so many cameras?"

Marcus chuckled. "You'd be surprised at some of the sneaky hooligans who manage to get in, but when the family isn't in residence, it's necessary to take precautions."

"Are you really related to the Hearst family? As in, the William Randolph Hearst newspaper tycoon?"

"Not me. Logan, my best friend since we were kids is the 'heir.' He's fourth or fifth generation, of course. It's a British name."

Caitey gave a tiny smile. "I gathered that."

"I noticed your vehicle was quite packed. Do you have something to do with the wedding?"

"Oh, yes," Caitey said with a laugh. "I'm Caitey Belgrave, Jenna's cousin. Our mothers are sisters, so our last names are different, but I'm the wedding planner. That's my, um, occupation."

He smiled again, and Caitey found herself gazing in awe at his teeth, which were absolute perfection.

"I've heard of wedding planners. It's a good idea since Jenna lives in New Orleans, but she and Logan decided to have the wedding out here. It *is* a lovely spot and more intimate and personal when it's a family home."

"I'm eager to see the house. I live in San Diego, so I'm in

the same state. Just had to fight the afternoon traffic, which is a bear."

"Ah, it all makes sense then." He sipped his drink, blowing across the top to cool it. It appeared to be hot cocoa with whipped cream.

Caitey wasn't listening very closely. She couldn't help staring at his beautiful mouth again. Not overly full or wide, but perfectly suited for his face. Perfect for kissing.

Good grief, where did that idea come from? She didn't usually fantasize about strangers. Not even movie stars, for that matter. It had been a long time since she'd fantasized about anyone.

CHAPTER 5

CAITEY

When Caitey lifted her eyes to his again, she gave a start. Marcus took the opportunity to gaze at her. He watched while her eyes floated across his lips and then rose to his eyes.

She blushed and picked at her bagel. She was taking tiny, careful bites and glancing about the room.

"Jenna hired you for her wedding, then," he said, pulling her nervous attention back to him. "Are you close cousins?"

"Oh, yes. Jenna hasn't always lived in New Orleans. We both grew up in San Diego. She moved there several years ago, and loves the history, architecture, and the casual lifestyle. She went to business school, then opened her own Coffee Loft franchise."

Marcus nodded. "That's what Logan told me when they were dating. Now, I'm curious why you suddenly ran off."

"You mean back at the house?" Caitey blushed. "Because you were *watching me*. Very strangely, I might add."

"Well, that's my job," he said with an amused grin.

"I was surprised neither Jenna nor the family was there. The place was deserted—except for the surveillance guy," she quipped, giving him a stern look from under her lashes. "You should have said something, you know!"

"I was going to," he protested, opening his hands in a show of innocence. "But you went around the back of the house and then zoomed off in such a hurry, I figured I had frightened you somehow. I decided not to approach you. Not when everyone was gone."

"Jenna texted me that they had car trouble and were at the mechanics. She suggested I come into town and get a drink. So, thanks for the consideration." She added, "You *do* realize that maintenance people don't usually wear suits."

Marcus let out a chuckle. "Touché! I hadn't thought about that. When I'm in work mode I always wear a suit."

She blinked at him. "Seriously? Why?"

"It's what I'm used to. I wore a uniform for too many years. And now I wear suits."

Caitey cocked her head at him. "May I ask what sort of uniform? UPS delivery guy? Electrician? TV repair guy?"

Marcus found himself leaning in closer, his hands cupped around his mug. She was teasing him, and he discovered that he was grinning. In addition to her professional dress and high heels, she was funny and adorable, too.

"None of the above, I'm afraid. I hope I don't disappoint

you when I admit I'm a retired Navy grunt. Special forces for part of it. . ." his voice trailed off for a moment.

"When you say, special forces in the Navy, what are you referring to?"

He gave her an unassuming smile. "SEALs."

"Wow," Caitey whispered. "I'll bet you have some wild stories."

"I'd tell you all my secrets, but they're classified," he said with a big grin.

She returned the smile. "If you told me, you'd have to kill me?"

"Something like that." Now they both laughed.

"So did all that dangerous, classified work lead you to this job. . .?"

Marcus nodded. "Yeah, I loved the Navy, actually and wanted to keep doing something similar afterward so I went into intelligence and spy ops. *That's* the reason the Hearst family hired me. I still do high-end security jobs for politicians and celebrities who are coming in for an event. You'd be surprised at how much demand there is in Southern California."

Caitey blew out a breath. "I wasn't expecting *that* but protecting high profile people does make sense. Do you like it?"

"Of course."

"Is it dangerous?"

"Sometimes. But I like living dangerously," he added in a low voice.

There was a slight pause, and he watched her finish her soda. Her body language showed nerves, but Marcus didn't want to make her feel nervous. His instincts were always to protect, serve, rescue, and help others.

He grinned, glancing at her plate. "Are you going to finish that bagel?"

"Oh!" She gave a little laugh. "Guess I wasn't as hungry as I thought. Do you want it?"

"Heck, yeah. I'm always hungry."

"I suppose tramping through woods and climbing trees makes a person hungry."

"I have a stepladder in the shed for when I climb the higher limbs."

He loved how her lips curved into a soft smile when she teased him. "Can't get your fancy designer suit dirty or torn."

"You better believe it. These nice suits the Hearst family purchases for my work are the only way I get respect," he laughed. "Honestly, I have a long reach, so installing security stuff is usually not a problem."

"Is there anything else you do as part of your job?" she asked.

"I also do bodyguard work. Living so close to Los Angeles and Hollywood gives me a lot of opportunity."

Her eyebrows came together in a slight frown. "I didn't spot a car. Do you walk back and forth from town to the estate? That's got to be ten miles."

"My vehicle was parked in the garage. I have an access code, and there are several parking slots. Usually, when I'm doing security at the property, I don't want other people to know I'm there, so I don't park my car or work truck in the driveway."

"That makes sense." She finished off her drink, making a slurping sound through the straw, indicating the drink was gone.

She gave an embarrassed laugh, and Marcus chuckled, too.

Her next question came out of the blue. "Did you follow me here to the Coffee Loft? It startled me to see you right behind me."

"Yes. And no. Logan called to tell me they were delayed. Getting a tire fixed. Jenna got on the phone and told me to keep an eye on you. When you took off like a shot down the mountain, I sprinted down the hill and behind the house to get my car and keep up with you."

Caitey smiled shyly. "That's nice to know they were worried about me. I sat in my car and texted Jenna when I got to the Coffee Loft, so she knew where I was."

"I'll escort you back to the estate if you're ready?" he asked.

"I suppose that's a good idea," she said hesitantly. "In case *I* have a flat tire," she added with a laugh.

"No more tire blowouts or car breakdowns today."

She rose and picked up her handbag. "I'm in the Nissan SUV just outside the shop."

"I know," he said with a smile.

Caitey gave a self-deprecating laugh. "Right. You literally

just followed me here. From now on, I'll think of you as 'security guy in a million-dollar Armani suit.'"

"Hey, it's not that bad," he protested, smiling down at her. "This is my second-best suit. I use it for outdoor jobs only."

"Well, you must be a pauper while you're at work," she said, her grin lighting up her entire face and dazzling blue eyes.

He couldn't take his eyes off her. But she was reserved and careful, which was smart.

"I almost forgot," he said. "Just remembered that Logan and Jenna want me to bring back iced coffees for them. She said that dinner isn't until seven tonight and they've been waiting at the auto place most of the afternoon. Will you wait while I grab those to go?"

"Of course," she said, waving a hand toward the order counter.

There was a lull in customers—only two teenage girls giggling in a corner were left in the shop besides them.

After ordering, Marcus pulled out his wallet to grab his credit card while Caitey darted forward, reaching toward the tiled floor. She appeared to be studying whatever she picked up quite intently.

She finally glanced up at him. "I think you dropped this photograph. Fell out of your wallet."

He froze for a moment. "Thank you," he said stiffly, taking the photo from her hand. Their fingers brushed and it was like that moment in the old movie, *Somewhere in Time,* when the past and the present collided and the world seemed to tilt.

The photograph was a wallet-sized image of his old girlfriend, a studio glamour pose in which her hair and makeup were professionally done. She wore an off-the-shoulder red evening dress, the same dress she had worn on the night of their engagement dinner celebration four years earlier.

It was the last night of happiness between them before their wedding plans ended, throwing Marcus into a dark and terrible world where nothing made sense.

CHAPTER 6

CAITEY

*W*ithout thinking, Caitey hurriedly scooped up the fallen photograph. It was pure instinct when someone dropped something.

Marcus was fumbling with his wallet and cred card while maneuvering the cardboard coffee tray to take back to the house for Jenna and Logan.

He took the photo without so much as a glance, stuffing it into the pocket of his slacks—*not* back into its place inside the wallet.

Caitey didn't ask who the woman in the photo was, although she was dying to know. The woman was beautiful and serene, with an affluent look about her that was instantly obvious.

Perhaps it was just a glamour photo taken in a professional studio, but she was certainly gorgeous, her makeup and perfectly coiffed blonde hair flawless.

Caitey glanced up into his face, but Marcus took care not to look at her. He didn't appear flustered, just incredibly calm and collected, despite how fast he hid the photograph .

No apparent embarrassment, but that might just be his training.

Maybe the woman in the picture was his sister . . . or a friend . . . or perhaps something more?

The late afternoon sun was lowering when she reached the Hearst Estate twenty minutes later.

Marcus pulled ahead to lead her through the gates— using a remote control device so she didn't have to key in the code—and around to the rear gardens and double carved doors.

After parking, Caitey grabbed her purse from the front seat just as Marcus opened her car door, sweeping his hand with a flourish.

"Milady Caitey, please let me escort you."

"You are too kind, sir," she quipped in return, careful *not* to take his hand to help her disembark.

The chill in the air bit at her cheeks. The crisp, pine-scented air of the winter forest sent a tiny shiver down Caitey's back. A comforting fireplace and the faint smell of spiced cider would be perfect.

It *was* November, after all, but three weeks before Thanksgiving. They were in warmer Southern California rather than the Sierra Mountains in the northern part of the state where it might already be snowing, but that didn't preclude the possibility of chilly weather or rain, especially this time of year. Most notably in the evening hours.

The wedding was planned for late afternoon, followed by a sit-down dinner inside the mansion where they could build a roaring fire, and nobody's teeth would chatter.

A surge of enthusiasm bloomed in Caitey's chest. This was the fun part. Putting all the pieces of a happy wedding together.

"Let's go inside and say hello first," Marcus said enthusiastically, carrying the cardboard Coffee Loft tray with the drinks he'd purchased for Logan and Jenna. "Then it'll be all hands on deck to help unpack your car. It won't take but a few minutes."

"Thank you, that's very thoughtful of you, Marcus," she said, saying his name for the first time.

Clutching her handbag, Caitey took a deep breath and walked up the granite steps while Marcus opened the double doors.

The moment she stepped across the threshold, Jenna knocked her over to give her a huge bear hug.

"You're here at last!" Jenna cried out.

Caitey hugged her back while Jenna whispered in her ear, "I can safely presume that Marcus took good care of you?"

"Of course. We just got a drink at the Coffee Loft. Thanks for suggesting it."

"Sooo," Jenna drawled, taking Caitey by the arm to pull her aside the moment Marcus slipped out of the room. "What do you think? He's very handsome, as is Logan, although you haven't met him yet. I know I'm talking like a giddy teenager, but I am giddy with love and my wedding!"

Caitey lowered her voice so as not to be overheard, omitting the details of seeing Marcus in the woods. "Well, of course, he's good-looking. I have eyes, don't I?"

Jenna's vivacious personality reflected a great passion for life. Her radiant smile lit up her face, which was framed by loose waves of blonde hair that fell around her shoulders. Her eyes, a deep shade of hazel, revealed sparks of fun and warmth, but also determination and strength.

"You smell like the Coffee Loft," Caitey teased. "I probably do, too, although I drank a soda."

Jenna rolled her eyes. "I love my little shop so much I swear it gets in my hair and oozes out of my skin some days. Is it that bad?"

"No, you smell cozy and sweet from all the sugar. I'll bet you're the perfect hostess, making superb lattes and teas while chatting up your customers with your usual flair and making everyone feel at home."

"I do love my job, but I love my wedding dress even more!" she sang. "Can't wait to show you," she whispered. "Girl time later tonight. Plan on it."

Caitey couldn't help laughing at her.

"Come meet Logan's parents. They own this place, but don't be intimidated."

"How can I *not* be intimidated when this entry hall is so immense and gorgeous?" Caitey whispered.

Her eyes ran along the glossy marble floors, the paintings,

45

the thick Persian rugs, and the 15-foot carved ceiling. She leaned closer to her cousin. "When I got here, I swore I had arrived at Manderley from that book, *Rebecca*. The wild, tangled woods, the narrow road, the sight of the mansion house bursting onto the scene."

Jenna grinned. "I see what you mean. Unfortunately, we *don't* have jagged cliffs overlooking the sea. That would be perfect, but there *is* a lovely pond behind the garages. We'll have to walk around the estate tomorrow while we discuss all the wedding details."

A tall woman in her mid-fifties crossed the marble floors on high heels. She had a slender figure and elegant shoulder-length silver hair styled in soft waves. Her eyes were a striking green, and she wore classic tailored slacks with a cream-colored blouse.

"Mother," Jenna called out, rushing over to give Victoria Thornton a hug. "Look, Caitey's here at last!"

"Caitey, darling, you finally found us on the mountain!"

"Hello, Aunt Vicki," Caitey said, relief at finally seeing her family after such a frustrating afternoon—even if there *had* been a little bit of excitement with stalker guy AKA Marcus Stirling.

She glanced around the foyer and the large drawing room beyond several impressive Greco-style white columns. Sleek, polished staircases curving upward to the second floor.

Her nerves returned. She had never planned a wedding at such a lavish estate before. Caitey whipped around to see where Marcus had gone, but he'd already disappeared. That was strange. Did he usually disappear like that? She assumed he'd greet everyone along with her.

Inwardly, she was amused. Perhaps there were more of those invisible cameras to install...

She couldn't think about the man any longer because her aunt swept her up into a warm embrace and Caitey hugged her in return. Her aunt smelled faintly of a sweet feminine musk and her fashion was impeccable.

"Here's your father now, sweetheart," Mrs. Thornton told Jenna. "He's been glued to the financial channel in our suite all afternoon. Your uncle probably didn't hear the doorbell when you arrived, Caitey, I'm sorry. I don't think Marcus even knew that Uncle Alex had stayed behind."

"Well, well, who do we have here? Two beautiful young ladies," Alexander Thornton said, appearing at the foyer entrance. He kissed his daughter's cheek before giving Caitey a warm embrace. "Hello, Caitey girl, I'm glad you made it here safe and sound."

Alexander was in his early sixties, tall and fit, with a distinguished appearance. His beard was short and neat, and he had a thick head of salt-and-pepper hair.

"Hi Uncle Alex. How are the stock markets today?" Caitey said with a grin. He was a financial planner by trade and loved to endlessly talk about investments for his clients—or potential clients, which was everyone he met.

He winked at Caitey. "I'm telling you; I have some great portfolios right now. Stocks were booming this morning but dropped off again. I think they should have rung the closing bell three hours earlier and then we could all have had a *rich* good night's sleep."

"Perhaps it's because East Coast time is three hours later than the West Coast," Jenna teased her father.

"Are you ready for this wedding, my dear?" he asked his daughter, fixing her with a meaningful gaze under a shock of hair that fell over his eyes.

"Of course, Daddy, I wish it was already my wedding day," Jenna teased back.

"Hold your horses. It'll be here before you know it."

"Don't wish it too soon! I still have everything to decorate!" Caitey piped up, and everyone chuckled.

Jenna turned to her. "We need to help you unpack your vehicle! You've been driving for hours, all loaded down. Let me find Logan and his friend, Marcus to help."

"You mean Marcus Sterling?" Caitey asked innocently, as if she and Jenna hadn't already whispered about him before her aunt and uncle had appeared to greet her. "The security guy?"

"What a coincidence!" Aunt Victoria exclaimed. "How could you possibly know the man?"

Caitey blinked. "We ran into each other at the Coffee Loft."

Aunt Vicki's forehead wrinkled into a frown. "I'm still confused. Wouldn't he have just been another coffee customer at the shop?"

"Well, um, he spotted me when I drove into the estate looking for everyone. After Jenna suggested I head into town for a drink, he recognized me, and introduced himself."

"He's Logan's best friend in all the world," Jenna told her. "They grew up together. Inseparable. And college roommates. Marcus Sterling is amazing."

"Oh?" Caitey said faintly, biting the inside of her lip.

"He'd give the shirt off his back to anyone," Aunt Vicki said. "Logan asked him if him to come out and do security during the wedding week. When you first arrived, did you happen to see him working? Nobody else was around then."

Caitey swallowed and pressed a hand against her side. A direct question couldn't be ignored; she certainly couldn't lie. "I did catch sight of someone moving through the trees, but I didn't know who it was until we bumped into each other at the Coffee Loft. He was . . . pleasant."

She certainly wasn't going to tell her Jenna's mother that Marcus was drop-dead gorgeous. Not with both her aunt and uncle staring at her with a boatload of curiosity flashing in their eyes.

"How nice is that?" Aunt Victoria said, clasping her hands together. "Fortuitous, and you had a real bodyguard to watch out for you."

"Is that necessary?" Caitey asked. "I mean, is there danger around here?"

Her aunt's laugh tinkled in the airy foyer. "Of course not, but since the village would have been unfamiliar, it's nice to see a friendly face."

He wasn't precisely what Caitey would have called "a

friendly face." Not when he'd stared daggers at her, watching her through binoculars when she arrived.

Caitey was saved by a tall, husky man striding in from one of the hallways.

"Here you all are!" he exclaimed. "What are you doing standing around in the foyer? Come, come, and have a seat through here. My parents have been eager to meet you all! With Jenna in New Orleans and me spending so much of my time there since we got engaged, none of the parents have met in person until now. Although at the moment, Mom and Dad have disappeared elsewhere on the property."

Logan!" she called out. "Don't get carried away showing off the property and gardens just yet. Come say hello to Caitey—my extraordinary wedding planner and cousin!"

Instantly, Logan whipped around, strode straight to Caitey, and gave her a huge hug. "Caitey, I've heard so much about you! I think you're Jenna's favorite person in the world."

"It's great to meet you at last," she said, overwhelmed at his energetic presence. Caitey could see how a woman would be attracted to him, and Jenna's eyes were drooling with love for her groom.

Logan Hearst was in his early 30s and had a stocky athletic build. His dark hair was short but styled, and his face was clean-shaven like that of his best man, Marcus. His eyes were a hazel color that radiated kindness along with a charming smile. His jeans and pullover polo shirt were casual, as if he'd been out tinkering in the garage on his car—not living in luxury on a multi-million-dollar estate.

"I beg to differ on the favorite person in the world," Caitey said with a smile. "I think that honor goes to Jenna's bestie in New Orleans, Marina Cormier."

Logan cocked his chin and eyed her in a mischievous manner. "Perhaps a tie, then. But blood is thicker than water, don't you think?"

"You make a good point," Caitey conceded.

Jenna leaned in conspiratorially. "Did I tell you the news? She and Wade are expecting a baby!"

"That's wonderful," Caitey told her. "I'm sure it's difficult to travel, depending on how far along she is."

"She's six months along, but they're determined to be here."

Logan waved them past the magnificent row of foyer columns and into an impressive great room filled with multiple sofas and chairs, lovely carpets, and wallpapered in gold and green from the top of the snowy white wainscoting to the high ceiling.

A grand piano sat in one corner next to exquisite picture windows that filled the entire back wall, overlooking the gardens, far lawns, and trees.

Beyond the glass, Caitey spotted beautiful patios, a pergola, a swimming pool, a hot tub, a pristine white gazebo, and the flower garden she'd sat in while trying to figure out where everyone was.

She followed behind, wondering when to retrieve her

luggage and unload her car. There were so many things about the wedding to discuss with Jenna.

She had never attended a private home wedding or over-seen a wedding in an estate house this regal and gorgeous. It was hard not to be intimidated. At least she had Jenna, and she knew her aunt and uncle.

Well, and Marcus, she supposed. A tiny bit. But he was an enigma, and she wasn't sure how much she could trust or rely on his help.

Jenna was such a casual, friendly, and down-to-earth owner of a simple coffee shop that seeing her here was also disconcerting. The imbalance had rattled Caitey.

That's what came from marrying a rich man.

Would Jenna keep her shop in New Orleans? Would she move to Santa Barbara?

Caitey had so many questions it was hard to keep them to herself.

Jenna leaned closer as if she could read Caitey's mind. "Isn't he dreamy? Come on, he's playing host right now, but you'll meet my in-laws soon enough."

"Any time for a cousin talk?" Caitey asked, giving Jenna a wink. "I only have a million questions!"

Jenna returned a secret smile. "Tonight. My room. Now follow me. I must show you the rest of the house."

"Remember, I need to unload my car. I'm sure everything is crushed by now after all day long."

"Of course! I get so excited about everyone arriving. We'll get the guys to help, and it will go fast." Jenna halted. "Hold that thought. Here come Logan's parents now. Oh, sorry, just his mother, his father is a trial attorney in Santa Barbara and will be home later for dinner."

A woman in her late 50s pushed through a set of double French doors from the garden side. She was carrying a bag of golf clubs and wearing a beautiful pair of white slacks with a deep blue blouse.

"There's a golf course on the property, too?" Caitey whispered.

Jenna gave a quick nod. "It was installed by the previous owners decades ago. Nine holes far behind the garages on the back acreage with bridges and a pond for golf balls to fall into," she added with a grin. "Quite lovely."

"We're fanatics about golf," Mrs. Hearst said, striding forward. "You must be Jenna's cousin Caitey, our famous wedding planner. We've all been so eager to meet you."

Jenna quickly spoke up. "Caitey, this is Mrs. Hearst, Logan's mother."

"Please call me Isabella, my dear. What a grand week we're going to have, although the weather is cooling a bit now that November arrived last week. We're spoiled living here, but at our mountain elevation, winter comes a tad early. But usually not until at least December," she added in a stern, joking tone. "So, no worries about Logan and Jenna's nuptials. It's the wedding of the decade."

Isabella Kensington Hearst had expressive green eyes that sparkled with humor. Her figure was curvy, and she was dressed in maroon slacks with a colorful cotton blouse that seemed to reflect her lively personality.

She immediately took Caitey by the hand and gazed at her with interest. "Has anyone shown you to your room, Caitey?"

Caitey shook her head. "Not yet."

"We will remedy that immediately. Before I forget, I'm assuming you brought wedding decorations and all sorts of fun things for Jenna and Logan's nuptials?"

"Oh yes, they're all in my car. That blue Nissan SUV parked in the rear parking lot beside the gardens."

Mrs. Hearst nodded. "Perfect. We will get these strapping young men to help you *tout suite!*" She rang a little glass bell sitting on one of the tables in the drawing room, and a gentleman in his mid-60s appeared through a side door. He wore an impeccable black suit, complete with a black tie and pressed slacks. He carried himself with the dignity of a retired military officer, and his silver hair was cut short.

"Yes, madame?" he said to Mrs. Hearst in a solemn British accent with a slight bow.

Caitey sucked in a breath, blinking at the grandeur of this moneyed estate. She stole a glance at Jenna and widened her eyes. *The Hearsts actually had a butler?*

In return, Jenna smiled sweetly and winked at Caitey.

Mrs. Hearst went on, "Miss Caitey, this is Reginald. He's been with the family for decades. In fact, he's like family. I apologize that he wasn't here when you first arrived. It's his day off, but we begged him to see us through the dinner hour and evening, and he'll be with us through the wedding. Maggie, our housekeeper, will take you upstairs to your room. Reginald, will you please organize these young men to unload Caitey's vehicle? Place all the wedding things in my study for the moment, and we'll sort through it after dinner."

"Yes, ma'am," he said. "Shall I require a key to get into the trunk?"

"No," Caitey said quickly. "I left it unlocked. The back seat is full, as is the trunk. And um, the passenger seat."

"Perfect," Mrs. Hearst said, as Logan and Marcus appeared in the foyer again.

Reginald headed for the rear French doors, Logan and Marcus trailing behind and making jokes. At the last moment, before disappearing through the door, Marcus turned to glance behind him and Caitey's heart jumped into her throat. What did that look mean?

His eyes on hers sent a shiver up and down her spine. Marcus Stirling was unlike any other man she had known. So strong and virile, plus confidence galore without being obnoxious. Just an hour ago, their conversation at the Coffee Loft ran through her mind like a blur. It seemed surreal now.

And that photograph that fell out of his wallet . . . Who was she? A man didn't keep a picture of a beautiful woman without her meaning something very personal and deep to him.

And yet, he frequently tried to catch Caitey's eye. For the present, she could not figure him out. Maybe he was trying to figure her out as well.

Caitey shook her head to get that last image of the too-handsome man out of her brain. He was attractive but not her type. Or so she tried to tell herself. Of course, the bigger question was: who *was* her type?

So far, the guys she'd dated at college had been mostly for fun, way too young to get serious with anyone, and all the relationships after college had ended up going nowhere.

No male had ever made her heart flutter. No man had ever made her look twice.

No man had ever stood out to her like Marcus Stirling.

Darn him anyway. Particularly since it was apparent he was already in love with another girl. He might even be engaged to that woman in the wallet.

So, she needed to ignore the guy, focus on her job, and create the best wedding ever for Jenna.

CHAPTER 7

MARCUS

*M*arcus was distracted while he, Logan, and Reginald unloaded Caitey's SUV. The boxes weren't heavy despite being filled to the brim, and it only took about fifteen minutes to empty the trunk and the car interior.

Everything was stashed in Mrs. Hearst's study, one pile and box at a time, while Reginald directed the best layout of each item and box.

"Look at all this stuff," Logan said with a chuckle, pointing out ribbon and tulle, and cut-glass centerpiece bowls. "So much gold and red with dashes of mauve and teal."

"Teal? Really? Never thought I'd hear my best friend use the word 'teal,'" Marcus said, giving him a hard time.

Logan snorted a laugh. "It's the popular new color, don't

you know? Get with the program. Jenna uses it all the time. She even painted a wall of her Coffee Loft shop in New Orleans a teal color. Said it was her accent wall."

"I guess shops and stores and—fancy mansions—all have accent walls these days."

Logan stuck his hands on his hips, nodding with a crooked smile on his face. "My mother is particular about her accent walls. Even the outdoor gazebo had to have an accent wall."

Marcus let out a big laugh. "Now that's going too far."

"It does look pretty good," Logan admitted with a shrug.

They returned to Jenna's vehicle one last time to ensure they hadn't overlooked any items.

Logan went to punch the button to lock all the doors, but Marcus stopped him. "Let's make sure Caitey has her car keys with her inside the house and not under a mat."

"Good thinking. We'll check with her." There was a moment's pause, then Logan said, "Speaking of Caitey . . . what do you think of her?"

"Um, why would I think anything? I barely met her."

"I know you too well. I saw that look you gave her over your shoulder."

Marcus shrugged, not wanting to talk about it. "Just making sure she didn't have any last-second instructions. Carry out a task, and the women send you back with forgotten items."

"Sorry, Marcus, I'm not buying it. Jenna was on the other

side of the room when you turned your head." Logan paused, then with a knowing smirk said, "Caitey does seem nice."

"Yes," he said noncommittally.

"And . . . you have nothing else to add? Jenna mentioned that the two of you grabbed coffee while waiting for me and my parents to show up."

"How would Jenna know that?" Marcus asked, trying to distract Logan, already knowing that Caitey had told Jenna she was at the Coffee Loft, and that Jenna knew he was at the Coffee Loft as well.

"Because Jenna told her to go there while she had to wait for Jenna and me to return from the tire shop. Caitey isn't an unknown hired wedding planner. She and Jenna are not just cousins but close friends."

"Tthat's true."

Marcus wasn't sure where this conversation was going, but he didn't want to reveal his intense attraction to Caitey Belgrave. It seemed too soon. The two of them had just met.

"We bumped into each other in town. She was locked out here while everyone was gone. Reginald hadn't arrived yet for the evening. Gus doesn't answer doors or telephones. I was doing security. We *just happened* to go to the same place to get coffee. It's the best place in the village. Although . . . now that I think of it, neither of us actually ordered coffee."

Logan laughed. "Don't change the subject. So, did you sit at the same table? Ignore each other? Caitey is incredibly good-looking. She seems like a poised woman, and Jenna obviously loves her. You haven't taken notice of anyone since Shelley—"

Marcus raised his hands. "Don't remind me."

"Sorry, buddy, I don't mean to bring up bad memories."

Marcus shrugged. "I didn't particularly notice Caitey's good looks. Well," he added with a sly laugh, "she does have excellent legs."

There was a moment of silence while Marcus hoped Logan would drop the subject.

Instead, his friend narrowed his eyes. "How long were you there?"

"Uh, I wasn't watching the clock."

Logan chuckled, shaking his head. "That tells me you didn't just order a drink and leave. You stayed. You got a table. You two had a little mini date."

Marcus lifted his hands to stop him. "We did not have a mini date. Caitey hardly looked at me or spoke to me. She accused me of *stalking* her, for crying out loud."

Logan took a step backward. "Come again. She *what*? Why would she think you're a stalker? What did you *do*?"

"Stop with the hundred questions," Marcus said, walking a few steps away from Caitey's vehicle and heading toward the stone pathways back to the garden.

Even though Marcus would be guarding the estate over the next several days, but didn't realize he'd have to guard his thoughts and actions from his best friend in regard to a gorgeous dark-haired woman.

CHAPTER 8

CAITEY

*M*rs. Hearst took Caitey's hand in hers, a look of motherly kindness in her eyes. "We'll get you settled into your room so you can take a break from all of us and unpack before dinner."

A woman in her late 40s appeared from another door on the opposite side of the drawing room.

"There you are, Maggie," Mrs. Hearst said. "Please show Caitey to her room and help her with anything she needs."

"Yes, ma'am, my pleasure."

Caitey blinked her eyes at being waited on. She was used to carrying her own luggage, but Maggie, the housekeeper, was a whirlwind of energy and efficiency. Her salt-and-pepper hair was pulled back into a neat bun, and out of nowhere, she had Caitey's suitcase and handbag in hand to lead her up the first set of beautiful circular staircases.

"Wait for me," Jenna called before hurrying right behind Caitey. She took Caitey's hand in hers and squeezed it.

"We'll let the men bring it all in, and after dinner, we'll go through the wedding things you brought and decide where the decorations will look best."

"Sounds great," Caitey said, following Maggie up the curving stairs and then down a hallway where there appeared to be bedrooms, bathrooms, and a lovely open sitting room with cozy, feminine furniture. She leaned in to Jenna. "Where is your room?"

"I'm right next to you, so no worries. You won't be alone. It's all kind of overwhelming, huh? But when Logan brought me here last year, I fell in love with the place and his parents, and I thought it would be the perfect place to get married. Cozy to be married at home, but infinitely more beautiful than a rented hall or outdoor venue in case of severe weather."

"But aren't you getting married outside?"

"We are," Jenna said in a sing-song voice. "The flower gardens are still blooming so lovely, and yet, I always wanted a fall wedding when the leaves were turning yellow, gold, and red. I got both. As I mentioned earlier, the dancing will be inside the drawing room. That's where most of the deco- rating will happen."

"We can decorate the chairs and the arbor in the back- yard, though. I brought all that with me."

Jenna clapped her hands in delight. "I can't wait to see how it all looks."

Maggie stopped at one of the white-painted beveled doors and opened it with a key taken from a jangling set of keys. It reminded Caitey of Mrs. Hughes in the *Downton Abbey* series, with her large metal ring heavy from all the keys to the manor house attached at her waist.

"Miss Caitey, please," she said, extending a hand. "After you, ladies."

Caitey smiled at Jenna as they walked inside a bedroom suite obviously meant for a woman. Mauves and pinks with dark wood accents in a large rectangular room with ten-foot ceilings. A broad picture window overlooked the gardens and rear grounds.

A four-poster bed with a thick comforter and tons of piled pillows sat in the center on plush carpet.

A sitting area, a desk for writing, and an ensuite bathroom through a separate doorway, complete with a shower, a separate tub with jets, and a long vanity for all her personal stuff.

"Wow, Jenna, Mrs., um, Maggie . . . this is gorgeous."

"Just Maggie, my dear," the housekeeper said. "Let me show you how all the faucets work so you don't get snagged while showering or dressing later this evening or in the morning. Nothing more frustrating than going to a hotel and being unable to figure out how the handles work, right?"

"So true," Caitey said weakly, following her into the large white bathroom with gold faucets, cozy rugs, and a double sink.

Everything was fresh and clean, and the suite was immaculate.

"I do the bedroom suites myself," Maggie bragged. "The housekeeper service that comes in weekly does the main house, but I care for the bedrooms myself to ensure they're done right. Especially for the lady folk."

"Oh my, there are fresh flowers on the bureau and on the small table in the sitting corner," Caitey said. "You think of everything."

"All it takes is a list and a keen eye," Maggie said, her smile growing into a wide grin. She smoothed her hands along the sides of her work dress. "I love checking off my lists. Doesn't everybody?"

Caitey laughed. "Me, too. That's what I'll be doing later. Checking all my wedding lists and making sure I brought everything with me—even though I checked at home before I drove up here. Even so, I worry every time that I've forgotten something."

"Human nature, my dear," Maggie chuckled. "Totally normal."

"Even if you forgot something," Jenna said, "that just gives us an excuse to go shopping."

"Are the Hearst's inviting anyone new that's not on my list of expected guests?" Caitey asked.

"Nope," Jenna said, her eyes going to the ceiling as she thought out loud. "A few neighbors and long-time friends, but only two or three couples. Logan's parents have a couple of siblings and a few cousins up in the Bay Area. They already sent lovely gifts in case they couldn't make it." Jenna said, her eyes sparkling. "But," she added, "I don't think they're inviting business associates since we decided to go smaller and more intimate. But everyone who is coming to the ceremony will stay for the reception dinner."

"Sounds perfect. You asked me to plan for about twenty, so that's the number of decorations for chairs and tables I brought, with a few extras for those 'just in case' moments. Oh! You were able to pick up the chairs and the arch for the arbor, right?" Caitey asked.

"No worries, they're all here!" Jenna said gaily. "We just have to set it all up and add the goodies—as in flowers, ribbon, etc! Of course, Logan still hopes his older brother and wife can get the time off to fly in from Maine, but they haven't been very optimistic. With two young children, finding childcare, and taking three flights to get across the country, they might not make it."

I will let you unpack now, Miss Caitey," Maggie said. "But if you need anything, you can call me on the house phone sitting at the bedside table. I'm available day or night. My name and extension are listed, along with Reginald and Gus, the cook."

"Night, too?" Caitey repeated in awe. Wow, a house phone, too. This place was like out of a movie.

"I live on-site in my cottage far back on the grounds. You can't see it from here, which gives *me* and the family our privacy. Reginald is also on-site, but the cook only comes in for weekends and special occasions. Mrs. Hearst does the weekday cooking. She took cooking lessons a few years ago and insists it's one of her hobbies and pleasures now."

"It can be a fun hobby, especially for experimenting with recipes."

Maggie headed to the door. "And now I will say *au revoir* until later."

As soon as the door closed behind Maggie, Jenna wrapped her arms around Caitey and hugged her. "I am so excited! I can't stand it. I'm getting married in less than two days!"

Caitey took a deep breath. "I hope I can pull together exactly what you want."

"I'm not worried about it at all. And if we need anything else, we'll just *go shopping*! Right now, unpack, have a lie-down, and I'll meet you in Mrs. Hearst's study before dinner to look through all the wedding stuff."

"When is dinner again?"

"Seven o'clock." Jenna grinned. "Sorry, I keep forgetting you're new here. I'll knock on your door, and we'll go down together so I can show you where the study is."

"You'd better!" Caitey threatened with a laugh. "I'll get lost and the guys will tease me to no end."

"Just in good fun. Logan can be quite entertaining. I don't know Marcus as well, but I've met him a couple of times before now when I was here visiting and first met the family last year."

"Um, Marcus can be intimidating," Caitey admitted, trying to sound nonchalant.

"It's the Navy SEAL regimentation built into him. Don't let him bother you. He's really very sweet. And," Jenna said, lowering her voice to nearly a whisper, "he has some kind of *secret past.*"

Caitey's eyebrows raised so high they were probably in her hairline by now. "Secret past?! Dare I ask what's all about?"

She hadn't told Jenna about the photograph of the gorgeous woman falling from his wallet. But this news was not surprising from Marcus's reaction to get that picture out of sight as fast as possible.

"I honestly do not know. Logan won't even talk about it. He said it was a private matter and not his to divulge. I told him that after I become his wife, he'd better give me a tell-all session. He and Marcus talk practically every day."

"Have you heard any rumors?" Caitey was now deathly curious.

"Nope. I haven't ever gotten any vibes from Mr. or Mrs. Hearst about it. If it was something major, they probably know as well, right?"

"It makes sense if their son is such a long-time friend of Marcus." She paused, then added, "His impassive face and erect posture make me think I should call him *Mr. Stirling.*"

Jenna laughed. "That's the military training in him. He's honestly a good guy. You have to get to know him."

"For now, I think I'll steer clear."

"Oh, Caitey, you're being silly. Since we will be together for several days, we should all be friends. Stay up late playing games, eating popcorn, and laughing ourselves silly."

Caitey gave her a small smile. "That sounds nice. I haven't done that since I last visited you in New Orleans a year ago! By the way, how are you and Logan making your long-distance relationship work?"

"He moved to New Orleans a few months ago. I thought I'd told you! I'm sorry," Jenna cried. "I've been busy opening another Coffee Loft franchise in the suburbs. Building, staffing, and the grand opening have taken over my life the past year!"

"I knew it would," Caitey said. "Have you bought a house together yet? I remember you saying that you were house shopping."

"Yes, and we're moving in after our honeymoon. It's being painted right now, and all our furniture is in storage. Can. Not. Wait!"

Caitey reached over and embraced her. "This is like an exotic trip for me, too."

"Okay, my beautiful cousin," Jenna said. "Take a break after your drive and craziness today. I'll see you in a little while at dinner."

When Caitey closed the bedroom door and sagged against it, fatigue slammed into her. A "lie-down" was precisely what she needed. Especially to get some energy back before dinner with everyone in a couple of hours.

The idea was intimidating. *This house* was intimidating.

The Hearsts were genuinely nice and welcoming, but their worlds were vastly different.

After unpacking her suitcase, hanging up blouses and dresses, and laying out her makeup bag in the bathroom, Caitey slipped off her shoes, climbed onto the gorgeous bed, moved aside some pillows, and stared at the beautiful four-poster damask hangings.

Staying here was like a vacation—except for the wedding work—because it was like living in a castle.

Just before closing her eyes, she realized she still needed to tell Jenna about the photograph Marcus Stirling had dropped at the Coffee Loft shop.

She strongly suspected the photograph was the key to figuring out that inscrutable, and puzzling, man.

CHAPTER 9

CAITEY

*W*hat seemed like ten minutes was suddenly more than an hour when a relentless knocking startled Caitey awake.

She sat up, completely disoriented. The late afternoon shadows had darkened the bedroom. But wow, the bed was dreamy and soft and perfect. She'd sleep like a log tonight.

"Caitey . . . Caitey, wake up!" Jenna was hissing through the door when she slipped off the bed and ran to open it.

"You fell asleep," her friend said immediately as Caitey pulled the door open.

"More tired than I thought," Caitey admitted with a wan smile.

"We both have had some crazy months lately. You did two weddings recently?"

"Yours is the third one this autumn season," Caitey admitted weakly.

"Yikes! I hope you got paid well. And I'm sorry I piled my wedding so soon after the others."

Caitey's lips broke into a wide smile. "Well, first of all, I received a very nice bonus from one of the weddings and went shopping, and second of all, I've been looking forward to your wedding the most, of course!"

"That dress you're wearing is beautiful on you! But we'll probably have to don jeans for the decorating party."

"True, true." Caitey's stomach growled. "Hope I didn't miss dinner."

"I would never do that to you. I remembered to set my alarm. I'm excited to go look at what decorations you brought."

"Let me comb my hair and freshen up first."

In the bathroom, Caitey brushed her teeth, ran her fingers through her thick hair, and then added a touch of color to her lips, checking that her mascara hadn't smudged.

When they arrived downstairs, Mrs. Hearst was nowhere to be seen, but she had left the door open to her study. The contents of Caitey's SUV were neatly stacked on tables and desks, but the heavier items were on the floor.

"Here, Caitey," Jenna said, handing over a glass of lemonade that had been on a tray on one of the open spaces of the desk. "I figured I wasn't the only one feeling parched. It's homemade by Maggie. I raided the kitchen before I woke you up."

Caitey took a sip and then another. "Wow, that's delicious. Just what I needed."

"Show me everything!" Jenna said excitedly. "Where should we start?"

"Let's discuss the ceremony first, then the outdoor reception. Any differences between the people attending the ceremony and the dinner reception?"

"No, everyone has been invited to both. We figured about twenty people and it's still about that. If Marina and Wade are here. Less if they don't make it."

Caitey rummaged through the first box, pulling out her detailed notes and a timeline of events. Her cousin rushed forward and tugged out a charm bracelet from the smaller box.

"You still have this?" Jenna asked, her face lighting up with amusement.

Caitey bit her lips, embarrassed. Would Jenna make fun of her sentimentality?

"Of course," she swiftly replied, trying to exude confidence. "A charm for every wedding I've planned and executed successfully."

The pewter and gold-plated or glass charms were all couples dressed in their wedding finery. The grooms with a top hat, the brides with flowing gowns and veils. Her very first charm had come from the bride as a thank you gift for planning a successful—Caitey's first ever—wedding.

The amount of work just about killed Caitey, but it was so gorgeous with no major problems, that she was proud of her accomplishment *and* the beautiful little charm of the couple. The bride had even painted their faces and eye colors.

So far, the bracelet boasted ten little silver charms. Jenna's and Logan Hearst's wedding would be the eleventh she had executed over the previous few years since striking out and building her own business.

Jenna fingered each charm, smiling, and then lifted her eyes. "This is super cute."

"Maybe it's just superstitious, but I think—I hope—it brings me luck. So far, ten out of ten have been pretty darn good—and all ten couples are still married. I consider that a roaring success."

"Indeed!" Jenna said with a small laugh. "It must have been the secret sauce in the cake."

"Or the rum!" Caitey said, giggling. "A major coup d'état of revenge after getting fired from my old job."

"Indeed! I love these silver bells you found. They'll look great lining the patios, like we discussed. Perfect for a fall wedding," Jenna said, digging into one of the boxes and pulling things out.

"Look at this ribbon. It matches the shade of silver and the mauves you wanted perfectly. I'll string it between the stakes with the bells. Which makes a better and more elegant 'rope' line than regular old rope, of course."

Jenna gave her a humorous smirk. "But not nearly as effective as actual rope where you can strangle the drunk guest making passes at the women."

"Quite true!" Caitey retorted. "I ordered the flowers for the arch that you wanted, twenty black, comfy chairs for the guests, a rug for the aisle, hanging lamps, and *lots* of tulle that I'll decorate with roses and lilies."

"When do we pick all the rest of it up?" Jenna asked.

"Tomorrow for sure, so we can get it all decorated. Except for the flowers, of course. We'll pick those up first thing on the morning of the wedding."

"I made sure Logan ordered my bouquet and boutonnieres for him, his dad, Marcus, and my father. I also told him to get one for Reginald, who will be our Master of Ceremonies, so to speak."

"Perfect!" Caitey exclaimed. "Have you given him instructions yet?"

"He'll usher all the guests to the ceremony outside, and then the wedding party into the drawing room afterward, and make sure everyone is seated properly. He told me—with a tiny, wry smile—that he would be honored. And I know he'll be splendid."

"He's like every British butler you see in the movies."

"I told you we've invited a few neighbors up here on the mountain, right?"

"Yes, you mentioned that."

Jenna laughed at herself. "I confess my head is spinning. Maybe I should start making lists like you do! The Hearsts have a few close friends in Santa Barbara, another one of Logan's old college roommates, and Marina and Wade, of course."

"When do they arrive?"

"They'll fly in that morning. Which is nice for them because they'll gain two hours in time, and the ceremony isn't until mid-afternoon. Marina still has a bit of morning sickness, so she's worried about being tied to the bathroom and throwing up during the festivities. Her doctor prescribed anti-nausea pills, although she's been using them sparingly."

"Do they know if they're having a boy or a girl?"

Jenna shook her head. "The two of them are old-fashioned and plan to be surprised. I'll bet the nursery will have plenty of antiques."

Caitey smothered a laugh and shook her head. "Too perfect. A wooden rocking horse, porcelain dolls, an antique crib, and furniture. I love it."

They opened the rest of the boxes of decorations and snowy white tablecloths, plus the crystal-cut centerpiece bowls they would fill with orchids and lilies.

"I'll ask Maggie to iron these tablecloths," Jenna said as a bell rang from the entrance hall. "Wow, it's already time for dinner. Don't show me anything else, Caitey. I want to be surprised."

Caitey had just opened her mouth to finally ask about the photograph of Marcus Stirling since she was dying to get the scoop on the woman, but she was skunked again.

She would have to wait until after dinner . . .

The dining room was magnificent with gold and green

wallpaper, a mahogany table, and fine china and crystal goblets for ice water and red wine.

Caitey ate the tender beef bourguignon, observing the rest of the group's banter. They all knew one another so well that she felt more of an outsider than she thought she would.

At least she had been seated next to Jenna at one end, so all eyes weren't on her while she attempted to properly cut her food and appear as refined as the rest of the group.

Mrs. Hearst turned to her. "How is your suite, Caitey? I hope it's suitable and to your taste."

"Oh, it's gorgeous. Such a beautiful room with a perfect view of the gardens. Even the bed is soft and cozy. I admit I laid down for a bit."

"As you should. You had a long day of driving."

Sitting next to her was her husband, Charles William Hearst. He had a sturdy build and a jovial expression as though he loved a good joke or two. His hair was beginning to gray, and his full hearty laugh matched his warm eyes.

Dressed casually in slacks and a dark green button shirt, Mr. Hearst appeared completely comfortable with who he was. An attorney who never got rattled. Even-handed with an approachable demeanor.

"Where did you drive from Caitey—north or south?" Mr. Hearst asked now.

"San Diego. Well, actually Coronado Island is where I grew up. Normally, my parents aren't too far away when they're not living overseas for my dad's job with the government, but I'm currently living in their house—the house I grew up in—while my father's working at the American embassy in Portugal."

"How fascinating," Mrs. Hearst exclaimed. "Are your parents able to attend the wedding when they're living so far away?"

"Oh, yes, they're flying in tomorrow evening," Caitey replied. "My mother is Aunt Vicki's sister so they wouldn't miss Jenna's wedding for the world."

"Coronado Island sounds like a great place to grow up," Mr. Hearst said.

"It was—is," Caitey admitted with a smile. "So beautiful and laid back."

Marcus suddenly spoke up, his eyes on her face. "You must be a beach girl, then?" he asked with a teasing smile.

Caitey blinked her eyelashes at him, quirking her mouth. "I was always at the beach as a kid, but now it's a treat. Once you become an adult, it's hard to get away for fun, isn't it?"

"Very true," Mr. Hearst immediately agreed. "Can't remember the last time I went to the beach! How long have you been a wedding planner? Our new daughter-in-law is quite enthusiastic about you."

"Jenna is completely biased," Caitey said with a laugh, and the rest of the table laughed with her. She finally began to relax a little—while trying not to stare too much at Marcus Stirling across from her.

"How long has wedding planning been your career?"

"Seven years now. I majored in business with a minor in interior decorating, which fits me perfectly. Besides, I adore weddings. They are such happy occasions. I admit I've attended more than my share over the last decade. All my college roommates, my older brother who lives in Georgia, a neighbor, and a good friend from high school are now married. At least I could capitalize on their nuptials," she added as a joke.

The rest of the table laughed at that, and Caitey was glad she could relax a little. This environment was so very different from how she grew up. But so far, everyone had been welcoming and friendly.

The only person she wasn't sure about was Marcus Stirling. His secrets intrigued her, even more so since his mostly quiet demeanor during dinner.

"That is very true," Mr. Hearst said. "Even if a wedding is stressful for the bride and her mother. I, of course, speak from personal experience, and I'm just the father of the groom."

Everyone around the table chuckled at that.

"The estate is the perfect spot for a wedding," Caitey said. "I visited Hearst Castle with my family when I was eleven, and then again during college with friends. I was sure that I'd been transported inside an enchanted fairytale. At eleven, I hoped to spot a princess around every corner."

Everyone around the room chuckled at her description, but the women nodded in agreement.

"The original Hearst home is quite a magnificent piece of real estate. To put it mildly," Mr. Hearst added. "We live as paupers in comparison. The answer to your question is yes.

He is my third great-grandfather. He had five sons, and the third son is my great-great-grandfather. I never knew them personally, of course," he added with a chuckle. "Their lives are as foreign to me as the king of England.

"It's beautiful, and the gardens and flowers are magnificent."

"We're lucky they bloom most of the year," Mrs. Hearst said with a smile. "The wedding is just in time to use it. Probably the last outdoor event we'll enjoy until spring. We do get a bit of snow up here in the mountains during December and January. Despite only being a two-hour drive from the ocean."

"That's part of the beauty of living in California," Mr. Hearst spoke up across the table just as dessert—crème brûlée—arrived. Served by stately Reginald in a crisp white shirt and cufflinks. "We get every kind of weather."

Jenna leaned in to whisper, "The cook makes this himself. You will eat so good this week that you'll put on ten pounds, minimum."

Caitey grinned. "I've been forewarned."

When she glanced up, she noticed that Marcus was stealing glances at her. He'd been doing that most of the dinner hour.

The man seemed nice enough, but she after the scare he gave her, she was uncertain of how she felt about him. And she still only knew a little about his background. But the attraction was definitely *there*.

Caitey touched her spoon to the dessert to break the

crackly glazed crust. Taking dainty bites to make it last longer, she closed her eyes at the cuisine's excellence. Better than any restaurant.

When she swallowed, Marcus caught her eye again and smiled at her. He raised his spoonful of crème brûlée in a toast toward her, and Caitey wished she could smother the tingling sensation of attraction running down her spine.

There was something there—some sort of connection—but she was determined not to give in to it. Marcus Stirling was still an unknown quantity, and there were secrets in his chocolate-brown eyes.

Did she want to know more? Or was that entirely too risky?

CHAPTER 10

MARCUS

*W*hen Marcus woke up the following morning, he found himself tangled in his sheets, one leg hanging over the edge of the bed. He'd slept poorly—which was an understatement.

Weird and crazy dreams all night long. He kept mixing up Caitey with *that woman* from his past. Why was his subconscious doing that?

Caitey was beautiful and exciting. A little shy . . . No, not shy. She was a bit standoffish. Well, that wasn't it, either. He was having a tough time defining her.

During the time they'd spent at the Coffee Loft, there was a wariness about her despite him trying to put her at ease. He'd failed when he exposed his presence in the woods by staring at her like a weird stalker. He had to work harder now to earn her trust.

When he spotted Caitey's pure, innocent beauty, her pale skin and dark hair . . . He'd halted like someone had shocked him with an electric wire. And after gazing at her superb and sexy legs, he'd lost his breath for a moment.

That kind of attraction terrified him, too. He was afraid of losing his heart again to the wrong woman. He hadn't been in any sort of relationship since Shelley.

Attending weddings was the worst. He was only here at the estate because of Logan. He'd do anything for this family. After all, they were like family to him—more than that since they took him in when his parents had a nasty divorce. While his mother worked full-time and tried to keep the household functioning, Marcus was often on his own.

Mr. and Mrs. Hearst often told him he was like a second son.

A knock came at his door, and he finally rolled over and staggered to his feet.

When he cracked it open, Logan was standing on the threshold wearing running shorts and a sweatshirt. "You ready?" he asked.

Marcus blinked. "Ready for what?"

"Our morning run?" Logan furrowed his brow. "Hey, you okay? Are you sick? Because you look pretty terrible."

Marcus rubbed his eyes, fighting the magnet of sleep. "Thanks for the vote of confidence, bro. Just one of those rough nights." He shrugged while Logan gave him a sympathetic look. "It happens sometimes."

"Are you referring to your past life as a Navy SEAL or something else?"

"Can I plead the Fifth?" He paused and gave a sardonic smile. "Or all the above? Let me throw on my shorts, and I'll meet you by the back door."

Logan gave a thumbs-up. "I'll grab my running shoes. See you in the rear gardens. We'll run the perimeter and check the cameras."

"Sounds good."

Marcus burst out from a side door connecting a hallway to the kitchen three minutes later and jogged to the rear gardens. Flowers continued to hang on to their stems, but he noticed that some of the bushes had started to shift into winter hibernation. Petals had begun to drop. This wasn't warm and mild Arizona, after all.

Good thing the wedding was happening soon, so Jenna would have her colorful garden photographs. Marcus had overheard Maggie say something about the wedding cake being ordered from a local bakery, but Caitey would decorate it with flowers and affix the cake topper.

He'd happened to spy the piece on one of the kitchen counters. A glass-blown heart-shaped arbor with a kissing couple created out of fake diamonds, the bride's wedding dress sweeping behind her.

A familiar pain tugged at his gut.

He pushed it away. No sense going there. Every time he thought about that, the anger dredges rose, destroying his peace of mind. It was long done. Far in the past. There was no going back and righting the despicable wrong that had been done to him.

"Hey, there you are," Logan said behind him, clapping a hand on his shoulder. "You're wandering around like a zombie."

"Just waiting on you, lazy guy," Marcus quipped back, attempting a smirk that came out more stilted than smirky.

They began to jog, running up and down the stone pathways of the gardens to warm up, doing a few stretches before breaking into a sprint.

It wasn't long before they passed a rectangular building that housed multiple vehicles in separate slots and entered the rear woods. Marcus pushed himself harder and harder, breathing in gasps by the time they reached the rear fence line.

"Hey, guy, wait up," Logan burst out seconds later as he came abreast of Marcus. "What's up with you? I thought we were running as a team."

"Sorry," Marcus apologized, wiping the sweat from his brow. "Got lost in my head and pushed myself to see how fast I could take it."

"Running from demons?" Logan asked, lifting an eyebrow.

"Of course not," he fibbed. "Just distracted, I guess."

"Okay, if it's not your mortal combat nightmares from your time in Afghanistan, then is it a certain young woman you've met recently?"

Marcus played dumb. "I haven't met any 'certain young women' recently."

Logan laughed and shook his head as their pace slowed to cool down.

Marcus stopped at one of the oaks, pulled out his phone, and checked the video feed to make sure there weren't any glitches or problems.

"If you say so," Logan said. "But I've seen some very specific glances you've given the wedding planner since she got here."

Marcus gave him a side-eye look. "Making conversation at the dinner table doesn't mean anything."

"If you say so. But I don't recall any conversation between the two of you, just a lot of glances from you."

Logan appeared to drop the topic of conversation while they spent the next thirty minutes making the rounds of the cameras below the house, then hiking back up the slope to the woods near the entrance gates.

"You see anything on the video feed from the last twenty-four hours? Jenna and I hope we don't get paparazzi trying to get in. Even though we're not personally famous, the family name still has a reputation for local interest. Jenna was stopped in town last week by an obnoxious reporter wanting details after he saw the announcement in the paper."

"That's too bad. Did it turn into an altercation?" Marcus asked.

Logan shook his head. "No, but she jumped into her car

and peeled off—from the grocery store, no less. Who knows how the dude knew she'd be there."

"Wow, bad timing. The guy was probably just a lucky roving reporter and spotted her. Nothing has turned up on the camera feeds so no worries."

Of course, he didn't admit that Caitey Belgrave was on the digital feed. No reason to. But he'd indulged that once. To see her pretty, puzzled face as she searched for any sign of life at the Estate when she had arrived yesterday. Swiveling on her high heels while he admired those fine legs of hers.

But the camera had also caught her shock—and real fear —when she spotted him coming out of the woods. Seeing that had bothered him. He'd been stupid to stare at her like that and make her afraid. He hadn't meant to. At the time, he didn't think he was in the open enough for her to actually spot him. He should have called out, but she jumped into her car so fast that it was too late to correct his stupidity.

Until he'd found her at the Coffee Loft. The question was, had those thirty minutes at the coffee shop helped her opinion of him, or hindered it?

She was hard to read. Reserved, cautious. Those described her well, but Marcus didn't blame her. He probably *did* look like a stalker.

"True," Logan agreed thoughtfully. "So, if you're not having Middle East war flashbacks and you're not checking out Miss Caitey Belgrave, what *is* on your mind? I've known you for too long."

Marcus let out a belly laugh. "No sense going there. The

past is the past, and that's where I want it to stay. I don't even think about it any longer."

Of course, he was lying, but he certainly wasn't going to do or say anything to spoil Logan and Jenna's picture-perfect wedding.

Marcus was so lost in his thoughts that he hadn't noticed Logan had stopped and was staring up at the sky. The air was quiet and still, hazy clouds shadowing the sun. Not even a sparrow swooped across the garden pond.

"Maybe it's because I'm sweating after the run, but does it feel like the temperature suddenly dropped?" his friend asked.

Marcus snapped out of his reverie and stared at the sky. "Yeah, I think you're right. It's getting cooler, but the days are shortening. It's November, after all."

Logan shrugged. "I checked the weather for Jenna, and it's supposed to stay clear for another few days. At least until after the wedding, and we're long gone to our honeymoon."

"Where is *that* anticipated event taking place?" Marcus ribbed him.

"I booked us a suite on a private island in the Caribbean. Somewhere in the Atlantic Ocean. Not telling where," he added with a sly grin. "No phones, no internet. Just sand, sun, catered meals brought in by boat, and Jenna in a bikini for an entire week."

Marcus wanted to groan. He was incredibly happy for Logan and Jenna, but this entire wedding week reminded him of his own loss—the week from Hades four years ago.

He pushed aside the sudden flare of anger and grief, and his thoughts immediately turned to Caitey while he tried to imagine her in a bikini on a secluded beach with a cabana of their own.

Okay, enough of that. Time to take a cold shower.

CHAPTER 11

CAITEY

*a*fter breakfast, Caitey met Jenna in the dining room to discuss food, cake, decorations, and the timing of the wedding day.

As soon as they were seated, Caitey heard a male voice through the doors leading into the kitchen.

"Who is *that?*" Caitey whispered. She didn't recognize the deep voice with a folksy accent.

Jenna glanced up. "Oh, I forgot to introduce you to Gus. He's the cook I told you about. He'll be here for the rest of the week because of the wedding and all the house guests."

"Gus made all that fabulous food last night for dinner?"

"Oh, yes, he was a chef and ran his own restaurant in Los Angeles. I think he was trained in Europe, but you'd never know it. I think he actually grew up in the Bronx, dirt poor."

The kitchen door swung open, and a short, stout man

peeked his head into the dining room. "Hey, ladies, I think someone's walking over my grave. Someone's callin' my name."

"Yes, we're talking about you," Jenna admitted. "Please meet my cousin, Caitey Belgrave."

"Pleased to meet you, young lady," Gus said with a slight bow and a wide smile. "I hear you're our famous wedding planner. Miss Jenna didn't want *me* to do her wedding, only you. But that's fine with me because I've got my plate full already—if you know what I mean," he added with a wink. "Full *plate* and all."

The cook was grinning from ear to ear. A jovial man in his early 60s with a rotund figure and bright red cheeks was wearing baggy jeans, a pullover shirt and holding a long spatula to cover up his splattered apron.

"Gus has a talent for transforming the simplest ingredients into culinary masterpieces," Jenna said with a dramatic wave of her hand. "His kitchen is always filled with the tantalizing aromas of his latest creations."

"I'm just a homeboy, Miss Jenna," the man said in a self-deprecating manner, but he was beaming from ear to ear as if every day was the best day ever. "Miss Caity, if I can make something for you or whip up goodies or treats for your room, just let me know. I'm always prepared to please the taste buds of the Hearst family home."

"Thank you," Caitey told him. "Do you happen to have any cocoa mixes in the pantry?"

"Do *I* have cocoa mixes?" Gus asked, widening his eyes.

"No need to ask twice. I am always prepared! The very finest of cocoa, with all the toppings and sprinkles and whipped cream to go with it. None of that artificial Cool Whip, either. Real, homemade whipped topping from the best cream lies right there in my refrigerator."

"That sounds heavenly. Whenever it gets a little cool, I think about drinking cocoa. Of course, where I live in San Diego, that's pretty much never. When I went camping with my family, it was always a treat, and my mother would pull it out to drink around the campfire."

"So far, we're having a mild fall, but if that changes, we'll bring out the finest flavors from the back of my pantry. Happy wedding planning, ladies!"

Gus swiveled on his sneakers and disappeared back into the kitchen.

"Okay, back to our lists," Caitey said.

"I can't get over how elegant the cake top is," Jenna said. "Thank you for finding the perfect one."

"The bride's gown and sparkling diamonds are gorgeous, and that groom is even more handsome—even if he's porcelain," Caitey told her. "At least that's what other brides have told me."

Jenna widened her eyes in faux shock. "Oh, the double entendre, my cousin. You are wicked."

She shrugged her shoulders. "It only makes me cross my fingers to find a good guy, too. But wow, are they scarce these days. Maybe I should start getting on my knees and praying! Nobody seems to want to get married."

Jenna nodded. "With Logan's background of a philandering great-great-grandfather and great-uncles—who are all long gone now, of course—all of which sure had a lot of affairs and mistresses, it's hard not to worry that it runs in the genes!"

"I do like Logan now that I've met him," Caity assured her. "He's very kind and seems like a happy man. His parents were so welcoming yesterday. I'd been nervous about meeting them and hoping all my past wedding fumbles and job catastrophes wouldn't make them leery of me."

"They would never hold that against you. After all, you're my cousin, but I never told them anything about your wicked witch of the west boss! That is water long gone under the bridge, girl."

Caitey gave a wry smile. "When I first arrived, I was quite intimidated, but this gorgeous estate is the perfect spot for your wedding. I must admit watching Logan a little to ferret out his nature, but he's so down-to-earth. Besides, he's constantly looking at you and grinning like a kid at Christmas time."

"Really? Well, that's nice to know!"

Caitey let out a snort of laughter. "As if you hadn't noticed!" She began singing in a deep voice, playing the role of Logan. "And I've only got eyes for you-u-u-u-u-u . . ."

"The feeling is mutual, believe me," Jenna said, laughing at her antics. "I never tire of gazing at him. How lucky that he happened to come into my Coffee Loft that day. We hit it off immediately and have been inseparable ever since. Our wedding day cannot come soon enough!"

"It will be here in less than forty-eight hours!"

"There's *still* forty-eight hours!" Jenna said, feigning shock. "More than that before we leave for our honeymoon!"

"Do you have one of those paper chains we used to make as kids for Christmas to count down the days?"

"Of course!"

Caitey burst out laughing. "Okay, I don't believe you. Let me see."

"I'm joking, but it is a nice idea. Instead of two chains for two days, I could put up 48 hours and rip one off every hour! And then get up in the middle of the night to take them off on the hour at the top of the hour!"

"Be sure to set your alarm!"

Jenna made a face. "It sounds dangerous. I'll be falling over with fatigue while walking down the aisle as if I'm drunk."

Caitey put a finger to her chin. "Good point. A tipsy bride doesn't make for a good showing to the guests. They'll be gossiping behind your back for decades to come."

"I wrote down some notes on where everything should go."

"I did, too. I was checking out the house after dinner last night. Let me make sure we're on the same page."

Caitey spread out her notes on the kitchen table. "Tomorrow is decorating day. I called the shop where I reserved a few more decorations in case we needed more, and they said they won't be ready until tomorrow morning. But that works since the wedding isn't until five o'clock, and the shop is only thirty minutes away. But we'll need the men to help carry tables into the drawing room for the wedding dinner, which will keep the dining room free for regular meals."

"Gus and Reginald will help, of course," Jenna said. "That part should go fast."

"I have the tablecloths and centerpieces for the tables, plus a set of three candles of varying lengths to put inside these exquisite glass cylinders I found that will line the path to the wedding arbor."

"Ooh, I like that."

"Roses and carnations and baby's breath to circle the glass containers for the dinner table centerpieces. I also got goblets engraved with your and Logan's initials. Every guest keeps one for a remembrance of the day."

"Perfect," Jenna said. "For the garden ceremony, I reserved some gorgeous columned posts to create the pathway to the top where the vows will be held, ending in front of the rose garden with the backdrop of the woods and blue sky."

"Oh, what about the chairs for the ceremony?" Caitey asked.

"Can we just use the black ones we'll be using for the dinner? They're folding chairs, so quick and easy to set up."

"Of course, that's what I was thinking, too. China and silver from Gus's kitchen, right?"

"Yes, he told me that Reginald will lay the tables, as usual."

"Perfect. When will the cake be delivered?"

"Tomorrow in the late morning," Jenna said. "That will give us time to add the flowers and the cake top. We'll store it in the big walk-in refrigerator, which will be perfect because it will keep the cake and the flowers fresh."

"That's a good idea since we won't have much time to do it the morning of the wedding. We'll all be busy getting dressed and doing any final touches to the decorating before the final guests arrive. I keep forgetting to ask if you confirmed the final details with the minister," Caitey said.

"Yes, Logan and I met with him last week. He's the family minister, going way back since Mr. and Mrs. Hearst were children."

"He must be ancient?" Caitey asked, raising one eyebrow in a humorous arch.

Jenna laughed, shaking her head. "I guess he was fairly young when they were kids, so he's about seventy-five but *not* ninety yet!"

"Hey, I'm going to head out to check my car and make sure nothing was overlooked when the guys brought in the decorations yesterday. Nothing left hiding under the seat or in a dark corner of my trunk."

"I'll go with you. Two pairs of eyes are better than one, as they say."

Jenna linked arms with Caitey and squeezed her hand. "I am so happy you're here to do this with me. It means the world. It feels like one of those adventures we used to make up when we were eight years old."

"So true!"

A couple of minutes later, they reached her car parked in the lower garden near the fence line, where the lawns became dirt before the woods began.

Caitey popped open her trunk and rummaged around, but it was stark and empty. Then she opened all four doors, and the two of them looked under the seats and inside the seat pockets.

"Found something!" Jenna cried.

Caitey lay sprawled across the back bench seat, sticking her hands underneath to feel in the darkness. "What?"

"A picture frame of you and me when we were kids . . ." Jenna said slowly. "I'd forgotten about it. Weren't we adorable back then? But why is it in the car?"

Caitey felt a blush rise along her face. "It's not for the wedding, of course! I brought it to remind me to check and see if you wanted to put up some pictures of you and Logan on the table with the guest book. I found one that's really beautiful. It wasn't on the official list but consider it an early wedding gift."

"Oh, that's a great idea. I have an album of pictures from the past couple of years of dating. Never thought about putting up photographs."

"We could create a collage against a background. Wedding guests always like to see the happy couple evolve in their relationship. Plus, it's fun when there's a couple of silly or goofy photos along with the professional studio shots."

"I'll put it together before I go to bed" Jenna said. "Won't Logan be surprised?"

All at once, a chill wind rose from the northeast. The oaks and firs trembled in a sudden gust. The driver's door slammed shut with a loud bang.

Caitey popped her head up again, sitting up in a hurry. "What was that?"

Jenna pulled the passenger door closed and gave a slight shiver. "Just a sudden burst of wind. Like a microburst. But gusting—and turning colder. Well, chilly, at least. After such a beautiful autumn, it's hard to realize that winter is coming. But it usually doesn't get *here* on the mountain until closer to Christmas!"

Caitey closed the rear door where she was sitting and peered through the windshield. "Look at the trees moving," she whispered.

The tops of the pines swayed as if a giant was shaking the branches, then suddenly stopped.

"I guess that's our cue to go back inside," Jenna laughed. "But what if that happens on my wedding day?"

"It won't," Caitey said quickly to reassure her. "I looked at the weather on my phone this morning, and it's predicting the same nice autumn weather. Cool mornings and evenings, warm afternoons. Until closer to Thanksgiving—which is still three weeks away. Just one of those freaky California things."

"California can be pretty freaky," Jenna said as they reached the back door to enter by the kitchen. "But New Orleans runs a competitive second. Logan and I decided to live in New Orleans—at least for the next year while my second Coffee Loft is built."

CHAPTER 12

CAITEY

"Oh, before I forget," Jenna added when they entered the kitchen and shut the back door. "It keeps slipping my mind to tell you—I've reserved a string trio for the garden reception."

"That sounds lovely," Caitey told her. "We discussed music, but that was a long time ago."

"I've requested they play Pachelbel's 'Canon' while Logan and Marcus, his best man, walk down the stone pathway and up to the arbor. Then I appear at the end of the walkway, and everyone gasps in awe, of course. But . . ." she drawled, slowing her words. "Um . . . before that . . ."

"What?" Caitey asked. "What did you forget?"

"Well, I, uh, bought a bridesmaid dress for you!" she said, her voice rising with enthusiasm. "Now, before you protest and say no, *please* wear it as one of my attendants. It seems weird not to have at least one attendant, even for a small home wedding. You are not just my cousin but one of my closest friends."

Caitey bit her lips as she blinked away at the sudden emotion. "Wow, Jenna, thank you for that. I consider you to be the sister I never had. I'd be honored to be your bridesmaid. If I can fit into it!"

"Of course you will. You never seem to gain an ounce."

Caitey grinned. "Hopefully I haven't after eating Gus's cooking last night and this morning! It will definitely be fun to dress up!"

"Yes! I fondly remember dress-up days when we raided our mothers' closets and put on their costume jewelry."

Jenna paused and then her eyes widened as she clapped a hand across her mouth. "*Noooo,* I never bought any wedding earrings! How could I forget to take care of that?"

An older female voice spoke up behind them. "Jenna!" Mrs. Hearst said. "Caitey! Are you in the kitchen talking about wedding details again? I'd love to be a part of it."

"As would I," Jenna's mother echoed as she followed Mrs. Hearst inside.

"Hi, Aunt Vicki," Caitey said. "We didn't mean to leave the mothers out."

"I know I'm just the mother-in-law," Mrs. Hearst said, "but us girls need to stick together against all the men wandering this house. Plus, who doesn't adore a good wedding? Especially for one's own son! One of the biggest days of my life, as well as Logan's and yours, Jenna," she added with fondness. "I couldn't ask for a better daughter-in-law."

Jenna walked around the table towards her. "Gosh, thank you, Mrs. Hearst, that means a lot to me."

"Please—Isabella!"

Jenna gave a little laugh. "I'm sorry . . . it feels strange to call you by your first name."

"I know we've only met a few times before now but please, no more formality."

Jenna turned to Caitey and quickly interjected, "Logan's parents came to New Orleans to visit us right after he proposed, and the ring arrived. That's when we chose a date. It's hard to believe it's here! I'm getting married *tomorrow!*"

Mrs. Hearst was nodding. "Your wedding is a beautiful event you'll never forget for the rest of your life. Please call me Mom—or Mother like Logan does. When he turned fifteen, "Mom" was no longer an option. It was 'Mother' just to tease me and sound like a British gentleman who graduated from Eton. And then his teasing happened to stick and that's what he calls me."

"That sounds like boys," Caitey said with a laugh. "My brother, George, as well as a whole slew of male cousins on my dad's side do the same thing. Drives *their* mothers crazy."

"Will your brother be able to attend the wedding, Caitey?" Mrs. Hearst asked.

Aunt Vicki shook her head. "I'm afraid my sister's son and wife recently had a baby and she's not up to it yet. Not to mention, traveling with a newborn is difficult."

"Totally understandable," Mrs. Hearst empathized. "Weddings are often difficult to schedule with big families."

"Speaking of fake British accents," Jenna piped up. "I've heard Logan do that British accent thing with you myself!" she exclaimed as if it had just occurred to her. "I'll have to give him a hard time—or force him to speak British to me all the time," she added with a devilish grin.

"After all, *Pride and Prejudice* is Jenna's and my favorite movie," Caitey told her.

Aunt Vicki turned to her hostess. "I must admit that being here at your beautiful home is like stepping into a Regency movie, Isabella. It's like visiting a British manor house on tour—except I get to stay in one of those divine bedroom suites. Plumbing and all of the indoor amenities included!"

Mrs. Hearst's eyes twinkled. "Don't forget—I'm only here by marriage. Shall we take this meeting to the dining room table where we can spread out more, and Gus doesn't have to put up with our chatter and giggles?"

Gus popped his head out from the pantry where he'd been organizing shelves and unloading groceries for the wedding breakfast and dinner. "Don't mind me, ma'am, just counting the eggs, so to speak, to make sure we have everything ready for the big day."

"You're such a dear, Gus, thank you," Mrs. Hearst told him, rising from her chair. "Even so, seeing what we're doing might be easier at the bigger table."

Caitey and Jenna quickly ran upstairs to their bedrooms

to get their planning notes for the wedding before returning to the adjoining dining room and the older women, where the four of them set up at the large table.

Being here again after the previous night's dinner sprouted Marcus Stirling's handsome, rugged face floating in front of Caitey's eyes. Mentally, she roamed along his shoulders and torso.

His suit coat showed off that masculine physique that made her entire body sizzle like bacon on a griddle. Add some fluffy, syrupy pancakes, and she'd melt like hot butter all over him.

When Caitey looked up, she saw both mothers and Jenna staring at her. She cleared her throat and stared down at her wedding lists, running a finger along each item.

"Everything okay, Caitey?" Jenna asked, a smile swirling along her lips—as if she knew what her cousin was thinking.

"Um, perfectly fine. Perfectly . . ." she stammered, blinking her eyes innocently. "Let's figure out where all the flowers will be positioned. They're being delivered first thing in the morning, so they'll be fresh."

"Perfect," Jenna said.

Oh, yes, Caitey thought, her brain returning to Marcus. The man was perfect in looks, stature, strength, and kindness. She tried to refocus her attention on the wedding plans, but her thoughts were scattering like a ball in a pinball machine.

Even so, she couldn't really judge *who* he was until she got to know him better. And *that* certainly wouldn't happen in the next two days. The day after the wedding, they would go their separate ways and never see each other again.

After all, she lived in San Diego, hours away from Santa Barbara. *If* that's where Marcus lived. Or did he fly in from somewhere else? All at once, she wasn't sure! What a ditzy daydreamer she was becoming.

Her daydreaming was one of her personal faults, but an asset when it came to planning unique weddings for her brides.

"I think I saw the men outside laying the carpet and the chairs," Mrs. Hearst said. "This table is already laid for dinner so perhaps our little meeting is done for now. Right after dinner tonight, Reginald will set it for the wedding luncheon. That will be one less task in the morning before the ceremony. Shall we go check on our husbands, Victoria?" she asked Mrs. Thornton.

Jenna and her mother jumped up to head outside, and Caitey slowly followed. She hoped the outdoor set-up was finished. The wedding dinner menu had long ago been ordered, and Gus was ready.

Her stomach tightened at the thought of running into Marcus. Before this puzzling reaction to that man continued, she *had* to find out more about that man and his past.

Trailing after Jenna, Caity sidled up next to her while Logan, Marcus, Uncle Alexander, and Mr. Hearst finished tacking down the plush red carpet.

"Ooh, look at that, Caitey," Jenna said in delight. "I get to walk 'the red carpet'! I'll feel like a movie star."

"I thought it was a great idea of yours. So much fun on your wedding day. Besides, you are a star! The bride! The woman everyone will be admiring."

Even to Caity's ears, her own words sounded stiff. Her chest heaved watching Marcus—not wearing his suit coat, but in a tight T-shirt that made his biceps bulge and his chest ripple . . . She abruptly plopped onto one of the chairs to catch her breath.

Purposely, she turned her head to gaze across the gardens to admire the beautiful roses, but the attempt didn't work to keep him out of her line of sight. The guys kept moving about.

Tinkling water fell like soft rain from the fountains. The tall glass cylinders etched with gold that she had bought for the ceremony were placed along each row of chairs, from the rear chairs all the way to the end of the red carpet where the arch was currently being assembled by Marcus and Logan.

In the morning, she would place a trio of white and gold candles into each glass cylinder that would be lit before the ceremony.

Her eyes betrayed her—because she had no self-control—latching onto Marcus, again, while he and Logan set up the archway where the bride and groom would stand for the ceremony. Gold and red royal colors. The entire thing would be covered in a cacophony of colorful blooms when the flowers arrived.

Jenna plopped down next to her, smiling with happiness

at how beautiful it was turning out. "Are you okay? You have a strange look on your face."

"Um, no. I mean, yes. Just going through the details in my head as the guys set up."

"You silly liar," Jenna said, laughing. "I know you too well. What are we missing? I won't go all bridezilla if we've forgotten something."

"No—it's all good. Everything is going to be perfect," Caitey said stiffly, ripping her gaze away from Marcus. "Not sure I can stay out here any longer. The guys are almost done. Except for the—for the—you know."

"Flowers along the arches and surrounding the candles we'll set up later?" Jenna asked with a quiet chuckle. She turned to catch Caitey's eyes, then moved a finger along her thigh all the way to her knee, pointing it straight to Marcus. "Or is it something—I mean *someone*—else?"

A blush rushed up Caitey's face. Her cheeks were probably bright red right now.

"Did something happen with Mr. Marcus Stirling?" Jenna whispered.

"No! No, not at all . . ." Caitey protested, but her voice trailed away.

"Spill it, girlfriend! Now!"

"I—well, I have to talk to you privately. About another matter. Oh, it sounds so furtive and silly. Never mind, forget it. My brain is just blowing up like usual! After all, I can't even eat the night before one of the weddings I've planned. Sleep is non-existent as my brain agonizes all night long."

"Now, that's not a good idea," Jenna chided her. "You will eat—even after dinner. Gus has homemade brownies in the pantry. Tonight, we raid them! Right now, *you* are coming with me!"

Her cousin tugged on her arm, and they walked around to the perimeter wall where the stone paving ended in the pathway toward the front of the mansion. Here there was a second row of goddess statues and a second small pond.

Jenna perched on a bench and pulled Caitey next to her. "The sun is dropping, and it's getting colder. I'm glad the ceremony will be in the early afternoon and short, so we don't all turn into ice cubes."

"There's a definite chill in the air," Caitey agreed.

When silence fell for a moment, Jenna burst out laughing, poking at Caitey's arm. "My stomach is anticipating that delicious dinner Gus is making, so spill it, Caitey girl. I have a sneaking suspicion this is about a man. A man named Marcus Stirling."

"Are you the bride or my psychiatric counselor?" Caitey said, stifling her laughter.

"Both at the moment. Did something happen with Marcus, or am I just pulling all these weird vibes out of my imagination?"

"Nothing happened. Honestly, really, nothing. Except he scared the be-jeebies out of me yesterday."

"As you can see, he's perfectly harmless. And *terribly* gorgeous," Jenna said, putting on a high society accent. "Of course, not as handsome as the groom, but then I'm biased . .

. Okay, I'm about to smack you if you don't spill that little secret making your lips twitch."

"My mouth is twitching?" Caitey asked, horrified.

"Well, I exaggerate, but you know what I mean. I can practically read your mind."

"Remember the Coffee Loft accidental meet-up yesterday, when you were all in town and I was stuck?"

"Of course. I'm rather good at remembering the day before in my life." Now Jenna's lips twitched with amusement.

"Okay, okay, smarty pants. Well, as we were leaving, Marcus pulled out his wallet to get out his credit card . . . and out fell a photograph of a woman. A gorgeous woman, prettier than anybody I've ever seen in my life."

"His mother?" Jenna joked.

"I haven't met his mother, of course!" Caitey teased in return. "But *no*, she was *not* his mother. She was no more than thirty, absolutely stunning. Like a model or a movie star."

"Hm. Was she blonde? Big green eyes. Like Marilyn Monroe or Vivian Leigh—except that actress had gray eyes. I think. I'll have to watch *Gone with the Wind* again sometime."

"Blue," Caitey said absentmindedly.

"How can you be sure?"

"Trust me. I've only watched *Gone with the Wind* about fifteen times. My mother loves it, and we've been watching it every year since I was eleven. But some people say that Scarlett's eyes were blue gray."

"I remember visiting you for New Year's when we were about fifteen and we all watched it together. It was my first time to see it and I cried my silly eyes out."

Caitey turned her head at the same time Jenna turned to look at her. Their eyes locked. Then they laughed.

"Okay, back to the *big* question at hand?" Jenna asked. "I don't know for sure who she is, but I've heard her mentioned between Marcus and Logan. After all, they've been besties since they were children in elementary school."

"And . . .?"

"She was an old girlfriend . . ."

"That's pretty vague. Why would he carry a photo of an old girlfriend from eons ago. Have you ever met her?"

"No. I met Logan two years ago, and this woman was from about four years ago, give or take a few months."

"Why would he still carry her picture?"

"It might be a mistake?" Jenna said vaguely. "Like he forgot he still had it."

"How could he forget a picture?"

"Maybe it was stuffed behind the credit card, and he'd forgotten about it?"

"He acted so strange about the whole thing. As soon as I picked it up and Marcus realized I'd seen the woman in the photograph, he quickly stuffed it into his pocket, followed by his wallet. A bit of red crept over his face. And then he pretended nothing weird had happened at all."

"Hmm," Jenna murmured, musing on the topic.

"If a photo dropped from my wallet or purse, I might

have joked and said it was my brother or an old friend. Or somebody robbed me and swapped out my wallet."

That brought a smile to Jenna's lips.

"Okay, spill the rest of the story before I shake it out of you. I don't know why I'm so curious, but it would help to know Marcus better. I don't know whether to keep my distance because I don't trust him or worry he truly *does* stalk women. I could wake up dead," she added with a self-deprecating laugh. "Okay, you know that last part is a joke."

Jenna turned to face Caitey. "Once more, I can honestly and unequivocally state that Marcus Stirling is not a stalker. Like I told you yesterday, Logan has known him most of his life. He knows his family. I've hung out with Marcus numerous times. He's a really *good* man. The best. I think, yesterday, you took him by surprise. We weren't expecting you for another couple of hours. And . . . Marcus actually didn't know you were coming. Logan and I hoped to surprise him with a proper introduction to my dearest, darling cousin. But, you know, flat tire and all."

"Okaaay," Caitey said, blinking her eyes at Jenna to give her cousin a hard time. "So, you wanted to set us up?"

"Of course not, but we figured we'd be here before you arrived. The best-laid plans didn't exactly work out."

"Prove you're not match-making. Tell me who that woman *really* is. I won't rest until I know the truth. Mr. Stirling has to prove he's normal."

"Okay, I will. You deserve it after the scare yesterday. But first, you tell me the truth—my sweet, shy cousin is wildly attracted to him."

It was Caitey's turn to laugh out loud. She bit her lips, glancing behind her, but all the men—and the moms—had returned to the house. "Okay, you win, brat. Yes, I find him incredibly good-looking. And sexy. And funny. And sometimes, I can hardly breathe when I watch him work."

"Now you're talkin', honey!" Jenna exclaimed. After their laughter slowed, she continued in a serious tone, a sad look on her face.

Caitey felt her stomach drop. "Now you're making me nervous."

"Don't be. But it's a sad story that affected Marcus horribly. I spoke with Logan last night and he said that it was perfectly fine if I shared the basics with you. Especially when I told him you'd seen the photograph in Marcus's wallet yesterday."

"Thanks. I certainly don't want anyone sharing confidences or secrets."

Jenna shook her head. "It's not. So. Here goes. Marcus was dating that woman. Her name is Shelley Woods. They met on a helicopter trip over volcanoes in Kawai, Hawaii. They were together for three years, madly in love. He retired from the Navy—because she wouldn't marry him if he were overseas most of the time. She said she'd worry about him so much she'd be sick. He finally relented and retired so they could get married and start a family."

Caity gulped and her throat tightened.

Marcus had been *married* before. "Is he still married?" she asked in a low voice. "Is that why he acts a little uncomfortable with me? Or recently divorced and worried I'll come on to him?"

"Neither," Jenna stated firmly. "Turns out Miss Shelley Woods was working a con on an innocent military member."

"A con—what?! How?"

"She pretended to be a lonely, young widow who was destitute. She poured on the charm, the seduction, and a big, detailed sob story. She lied and said she was widowed so Marcus couldn't look up a potential ex-husband."

"Records are pretty easy to find, though."

"She told him she'd been living in Turkey with her pretend husband, who was also in the military, and the records were impossible to track down. She had the military spouse lingo down pat. Turns out she had a best friend who *was* a military spouse and worked as the Ombudsman on a naval ship."

Caitey couldn't believe what she was hearing. Her stomach felt sick.

"The wedding was all planned. A honeymoon to Bali all paid for. Marcus had booked a house on a private beach. Their own staff, a chef, housekeepers. He got her a giant 3-carat diamond, which she drooled over like a teenager. They joined bank accounts and were about to purchase a home together . . ."

Jenna trailed off, and Caitey blurted, "Don't stop now! *What happened?* You have me on the edge of my seat!"

"On the day of the wedding—at the church Marcus grew up in—with all of his family and friends and neighbors, the organ playing . . . Marcus looking incredibly delicious waiting near the minister for Shelley's big entrance . . . and nothing."

"What do you mean, 'nothing'?"

"The first clue that something was wrong was when it was fifteen minutes past when the ceremony should have started, but everyone assumed it was Shelley still getting all dolled up like the model she was and dressing for a grand entrance. Marcus didn't think too much of it at the time because his best man—Shelley's brother—was having trouble with the rented tuxedo in the dressing room of the church—at least that's what his father said. At first."

"I'm dying of curiosity and dreading the worst," Caitey whispered, eyes glued on Jenna's face.

"Well! Shelley was what they call a no-show bride."

Caitey blinked, trying to take in what she was saying. "*She left him at the altar?!*"

"Yep."

"Was it the best man who came out to tell him the news?"

"Nope. He was gone, too. Both of them disappeared. Literally vanished. Nobody has ever seen either of them since. Logan assumes they changed their names. It was all planned, of course. Multiple passports, multiple bank accounts. Heck, we don't even know if Shelley Woods is her real name. I'm sure she and her 'boyfriend' are off somewhere else, pulling another con on a new, unsuspecting victim."

"How horrible," Caitey said, her voice hoarse with sudden emotion.

"Oh, it gets worse," Jenna said cynically. "She cleaned out all the bank accounts. The brother who was the fake best man was not her brother at all. He was her lover and had been for years."

"The entire thing was planned from the beginning?"

"Oh, yes. She knew just what to do and say and tell an unsuspecting *good* man to get him to fall in love with her—and then take him for all he was worth."

"Being military, did he really have that much, though? He wasn't even thirty years old when this happened. Navy guys don't make that much to build a nest egg that quickly."

"True, although Marcus is good at saving . . . No, the most important thing is that his grandparents left him an *exceptional* inheritance when he turned twenty-five. She stole it all."

"Ah," Caitey said softly, a hitch in her voice. "It all makes sense."

"It was horrible. A nightmare. What can anyone say about Marcus? He's skittish, and it's taking him a while to trust. He hasn't dated anyone since. But . . . I think that is about to change."

"Why would you say that? Do you have some other female guests attending tomorrow you want to hook him up with?"

Jenna shook her head, laughing. "No, silly. BUT!" she added, staring straight into Caitey's eyes. "I feel vibes coming from the two of you. You're both trying to hide it. In fact, you can't stop being annoyed at him."

"I'm not annoyed," Caitey protested.

"You won't look at him. You're pretending he doesn't exist, but I know you, and you're lying to yourself. 'The lady doth protest too much, methinks.'"

"Okay, okay, I'm not protesting too much, and I know he exists! Who could *not* see the man exists? He's kind of, you know, nice . . ."

"Nice? Come on, girl."

"Okay, he's wow. Wow! With a capital W. Especially when he builds things. And climbs trees. And other things."

"So, stop avoiding him, sweetie," Jenna said softly. "He's trying not to scare you off. He knows you didn't have a particularly good introduction."

"Ya think?" Caitey leaned forward, staring at her cousin. "And, by the way, Miss Jenna Thornton, soon to be Mrs. Logan Hearst . . . how do you know these things about his feelings? Or my feelings? Have you been talking behind my back?"

"Of course not. Logan mentioned it. He can see it, too, even if you and Mr. Stirling are denying it."

"Good grief, I'm overwhelmed by that horrible story. Poor Marcus. What a nightmare. She destroyed his trust in anyone else." Caitey rubbed at the goosebumps rising on her arms. "At the moment, I'm getting cold. Isn't it time for dinner?"

"Yes, on both counts. Bottom line, dear Caitey. Give the man a chance. At least be friends. Don't be afraid of him. He wouldn't hurt a fly. Well, unless you're the enemy with a hand grenade, then he'll take you out flat in half a second."

Caitey smiled, shaking her head at Jenna's dramatic words. "I promise I won't avoid him any longer."

"Thank you. He deserves a nice girl like you. Now. Tomorrow, after the ceremony and dinner, I want to put music on, roll up the carpets, and *dance.* And then, Logan and I will disappear into the sunset. I've dreamed about the bride and groom dance since I saw it on TV as a kid. Some wedding show I can't even remember now. But that romantic dance stuck in my head."

"And you shall have it," Caitey assured her.

"Thank you," Jenna said softly. "By the way, when does your parents' flight arrive?"

"Mom flew in from Portugal yesterday, but the best flight was into San Francisco—after a plane transfer in Atlanta. She's hanging out in San Francisco for tonight to adjust to the jet lag and waiting for my dad's flight to come in late tonight. So tomorrow they'll catch an early flight to LAX. They should be here by mid- to late morning. Just in time. Of course, the wedding isn't until five o'clock, so it works out great."

"Perfect," Jenna said, bouncing in her seat. "How do they like their ambassadorship in Portugal? It's so wild to me that your father is a diplomat. Maybe he can give us the latest scoop on international relations and all the gossip, haha."

Caity laughed at that. "Yeah, right. It's all pretty boring. He and Mom go to lots of parties and state dinners, but Dad's days are filled with meetings upon meetings. Not very glamorous."

"I can't wait to travel with Logan. We have so many dream trips on our bucket list."

"Bucket lists are for retirement!"

Jenna sighed. "True, but why wait until you have arthritis? Oh, I can't believe it's happening. *My dream wedding to the man of my dreams is coming true in only twenty-four hours!*"

Laughing at her, Caitey rose from the stone bench. It struck her that she was chilled to the bone. Her entire backend was like ice.

When she and Jenna dashed for the back door, Caitey swore she spotted the shadowed outline of a tall male figure retreating from the window.

The window had been cracked a few inches, but whoever had been standing there shut it and pulled the drapes closed.

She was positive it was Marcus. Had he heard their conversation about his sad love story? Caitey was still shocked that the man had gone through something so horrible and tragic.

No wonder he was awkward around other women. After such a betrayal, a person could hardly trust anyone quickly again. It would take some time, a lot of time.

But she certainly didn't want him thinking they were

gossiping about him or the horrible things he'd gone through. His past trauma just made Caitey want to comfort him, to sympathize—and yes, she wanted to be in his arms, too.

She stepped aside to let Jenna go inside first, and just as Caitey was about to step inside the French doors, she turned back for a moment just as the sun sank below the tree line, creating shadows among the rose garden and the alabaster Roman goddesses.

The air was so quiet and peaceful as if she were somewhere quite magical.

But before she reached the back door, Caitey swore a tiny white snowflake hit her nose.

A snowflake? That was impossible. This perfect fall weather was supposed to last for three more weeks.

Caitey told herself that it was just a tiny flake falling from a stray cloud. Even if it rained a little, the garden would be fresh and clean and the small storm would be over by morning. Only the carpets and chairs were set up. The padded seat covers still had to be attached, the archway decorated, and the candles lit. There was plenty of time to wipe down damp chairs and let things dry out before the afternoon.

No, Caitey would not let a light rain shower spoil *this* wedding. Optimism was the name of the game! This wedding was going to be spectacular. The most significant gift she could give to Jenna and Logan, her cousin's true love.

CHAPTER 13

MARCUS

*M*arcus had gone to sleep listening to the patter of light raindrops against the windowpane in his bedroom.

The soft, soothing sound reminded him of the times when he was a newly enlisted Navy grunt before he began his SEAL training and had to teach himself to sleep on a ship in any weather, or any noise.

Now, the sound of a banging fist nearly took down his bedroom door. Or was that part of the dream he was having about Caitey Belgrave?

Now, where did that come from? He had to admit that he found her extremely attractive, kind, and sweet, although sometimes distant. Marcus determined he needed to find out why.

His eyes always lingered on her perfect figure, those

fantastic legs, and the elegant way she walked. *Those lips—her lips.* That mouth of hers needed kissing. Badly. But only by him, of course, he mused selfishly.

The banging on his door startled his sleep again—just like his commander used to do, barging in and yanking him out from under the warm blanket?

"Marcus! Wake up!"

Somebody pulled at his feet, and instantly he jerked awake. The fantastic dreams about Caitey fled. The bedroom he was lying in was still in shadow; the curtains pulled across the windows. Where was he? What time was it? Unfortunately, he couldn't see the clock through his blurry eyes.

Man, he hated that disoriented feeling whenever he woke up in a new place. Especially when rudely awoken.

He didn't have to wait long before Logan growled in his face and threw off the blankets. "Get your derriere in gear, sailor; we got work to do."

Marcus got up on one elbow, shaking sleep from his eyes, then dropped back to his pillow again, running both hands through his hair. He used to dream about Shelley, but those were never dreams, merely nightmares. after she robbed him and disappeared into the ether with her conman.

Good riddance, even if it had hurt more than he'd imagined. Love had turned to hate. The deceit was hard to get over and even more complicated trying to understand why.

Logan gave him a year to mope, then started his weekly ritual of bugging him to ask someone new on a date. He had not been enthusiastic for a long time. Having the rug pulled out from underneath you, having your life, your heart, and your savings ripped into shreds was an intense thing to come back from.

He was a zombie for months in the land of the living.

Then, one day, he finally grew sick of his lazy, unmotivated, unshaven self—with the help of Logan, who'd given him more than a few yanks around the neck—and slowly returned to the real world.

"Marcus, you in there?" Logan said now, a little gruff. "Can you hear me?"

He finally jerked to a sitting position, staring at the clock on the bedside table, which read a few minutes after nine. Wow, he never slept this late, not even on vacation.

The dream hovered and Marcus was desperate to drop back into sleep. Caitey was beautiful, sexy, and had a great smile when she wasn't so worried about the wedding.

He imagined her drifting through the ceiling like an angel, her hair billowing around her shoulders, hovering over him until she sank into his arms, where he held her close, and their bodies fit perfectly together.

"Hey, is that the actual time?" he finally asked when Logan entered the room.

"Yeah," Logan said, picking up a pillow from the floor and throwing it at his face. "And it's kind of a big day, you doofus. *My wedding day!*"

WEDDING!? That jerked Marcus into action. He sat up and pushed off the blankets. "Why didn't you wake me up sooner?"

Marcus's consciousness finally came fully into focus.

"You have a goofy smile on your face, sailor!" Logan said with a laugh. "It's *my* wedding day, not yours." When Marcus growled at him, his friend quickly apologized. "Sorry, I didn't mean it like that. I know that's still a sore point."

"You'd think it wouldn't be such a tender spot after four years. And it isn't. My hurt turned to hate, followed by ambivalence, and then anger for being so taken in by her."

"Quit blaming yourself," Logan chided. "But someone put that smile on your face. Might it be Jenna's cousin? Our cute and flustered wedding planner?"

"Mind your own business," Marcus said, trying not to laugh.

"If you want to make a move, now is the time before she leaves tomorrow. Well, *after* the ceremony, when Jenna and I are safely on our honeymoon. But we've got a big problem right now."

Marcus sat up, pushing the blankets away. He was on duty now. The old training kicked in, but Logan's following words almost knocked him off his feet.

"Hey, I'll check all the cameras right away. I saw the wedding announcement on the local news, and we might get gawkers."

"No gawkers this morning."

"Huh? How can you be so sure?"

"Because there's three feet of snow out there!"

"Snow! But I heard rain right after midnight."

"Temps dropped from sixty to thirty—and that rain

turned to snow. It's been coming down like a blizzard for about six hours. We're all on shovel duty. Guests will start arriving soon after five for the six o'clock ceremony."

Marcus rubbed at his jawline, still trying to shake himself fully awake. He didn't admit it to Logan, but of course, he had been dreaming of Caitey. And it was a *very* nice dream . . . She was serving him hot cocoa loaded with whipped cream, and they were sharing sips from the super-sized mug at the Coffee Loft.

But for now, he needed to focus. He cleared his throat. "So, um, we need to clear the entrance road and the driveway."

Logan shook his head. "No way to clear the road—not a quarter of a mile piled with three feet. We'd need a snow-plow. But yeah, the driveway, the patios and porches, and at least parking spots."

"I'm right there with you," Marcus told Logan. "Bummer about the snow on your wedding day. Have you talked to Jenna yet?"

"Just briefly. She sounded a little upset but was putting on a brave face for me. Her mother is with her, and they're figuring out a new battle plan."

"Wedding still on?"

"No question about that! I've already been waiting too long to marry Jenna. It's today. Or else, this man will be carrying her off into the wilds and finding us a cabin."

"Hey, that might be better in the long run," Marcus joked.

"But I promised Jenna she would have her dream wedding . . . so there's that." He gave a shrug and a wan smile.

Marcus nodded. "Yeah, I got you on that point. A woman must have her dream nuptials. Don't jinx it by denying her that on Day One of your marriage."

"See you in five," Logan said, then shut the bedroom door behind him with a firm bang.

Marcus jumped up, chuckling to himself. Thankfully, he'd come prepared, knowing this event was in the mountains. Within minutes, he wore long johns, a flannel button-down, jeans, a scarf, and a heavy coat. And thick gloves.

After he was dressed and outside, he and Logan retrieved shovels from the outdoor garden shed and began moving snow. Reginald had unlocked one of the garages and rode out on a snow blower.

Marcus whooped. "Now that's what I'm talking about," he called out to Reginald, stiff in a thick coat and knitted cap, and collar up since it was still lightly snowing.

Giving a salute as he passed, the older man drove the snow blower to the front driveway while Marcus and Logan fist-pumped into the air. That machine would save them a ton of work hours—and they didn't have hours. But the property was huge, and this would take a few hours.

He and Logan stayed in the large courtyard area behind the house, removing every speck of snow from the stones, the outdoor furniture, the Roman statues, and the flower gardens, which were looking very stressed—brown and sagging. Poor roses and lilies. It had been a mild autumn, but overnight, it turned to deep January cold and snow.

"At least a storm up here doesn't affect LAX."

"That's true," Logan agreed. "We do have a few more people flying in. Caitey's parents, for instance. I think they landed this morning."

Knowing that Caitey's father was an ambassador made her backstory to Marcus even more intriguing. Had she ever lived in Portugal with them?

He couldn't help thinking about the woman while he mindlessly shoveled and threw piles of snow into the yard area, away from the courtyard and main walkways that would be used from the parking area to the house.

What was she doing right now . . . Had she and Jenna gone into full panic mode over the unexpected three feet of snow?

CHAPTER 14

CAITEY

Caitey rolled over in bed and then sat up with a start. The room was cold. Noticeably colder than yesterday. She grabbed the extra blanket from the end of her bed, wrapped it around her shoulders, and checked the thermometer on the wall next to the bathroom.

It was only sixty-one degrees in the bedroom. No wonder she was freezing!

She pressed a few buttons to turn up the heat and stood under one of the overhead vents, but she couldn't stand there indefinitely while the room slowly warmed. A hot shower would do the trick much faster.

Rummaging through the closet where she'd hung up her clothes, she grabbed a pair of jeans, socks, and sneakers. This morning was furniture moving day in the drawing room for the ceremony and food prep.

Guests would begin arriving in just a few hours! The blue dress she'd worn yesterday wouldn't do for all the physical labor.

Before she arrived, Jenna had hung up the bridesmaid dress Caitey would wear in her guest room's wardrobe. She ran a hand down the satin bodice, admiring the deep burgundy color and lovely bodice lace.

It was floor-length and absolutely beautiful—princess-like, in fact. It reminded her of all those "dress-up" days she and Jenna had enjoyed as little girls, complete with crowns and cheap jewelry—and lots of giggling and delight. Of course, there was no crown today! But a set of burgundy and fake diamond jewelry—earrings and a necklace—fit perfectly with the dress.

It was so weird to remember their childhood. More than two decades had passed since those idyllic and distant days, but there were many fond memories. And now Jenna was getting married! It didn't seem possible.

Caitey turned on the shower to heat the water and jumped in to get cleaned up quickly. After finishing in the warm water, she wrapped the towel around her and hunted for a blow dryer in the bathroom vanity drawers. The bedroom was still chilly, causing her to shiver slightly.

And then Caitey remembered those tiny pricks of icy raindrops she had felt on her face last night.

Striding across the room, she yanked back the curtains from the picture window. The sight in front of her eyes revealed a cold, cloudy, foggy day without a speck of sunlight

... above a world of blinding white—a literal *blanket* of pure white snow.

Snow. Snow?! How did that happen? Yesterday was so lovely. Jenna was supposed to have the perfect autumn wedding, not winter!

Jenna pressed her nose against the cold glass. Not just a little bit of snow. PILES OF SNOW. A blizzard swooped in while they slept!! Noooo! She had to get a move-on, find Jenna, and figure out this wedding! Three feet of snow changed everything.

Hopefully her parents had retrieved their rental car and were on their way up. She hoped they saw the weather forecast last night and had made it an early morning, checked out of their hotel right away, and were already downstairs. Not taking any chances of being late due to the snow and road conditions.

Caitey tried to breathe. All would be well. It had to be.

Her phone buzzed repeatedly as she ran from the window to snatch up her phone still sitting on the night table by the bed.

Text messages were pouring in.

The first came at dawn from Jenna: **A snowstorm assaulted my wedding day! How did we miss this? Did we ever come up with a contingency plan? I'm so discombobulated, I can't remember!**

Caitey typed back: **Yes, the plan is just to move the dinner reception inside instead of the rose garden. It will all work out. Promise!** she added with all the enthusiasm and optimism she could muster. Jenna must be going out of her mind with stress and worry. **Meet you downstairs for breakfast in twenty minutes!**

The following three messages were from her mother. She had missed the one sent about midnight.

Dad arrived in LAX late, late, late tonight. Flight was delayed. Too tired to drive up to the Hearst Estate. We got a hotel room. See you in the morning, sweetheart.

Then came the sad news:

We picked up our rental car first thing this morning and heard from the Hertz agent that there was snow in the mountains. What's it like up there? Is it very much? Do we need to rent chains for the tires? I'm sure Jenna is highly disappointed.

The last message from her mother beeped as Caitey was reading.

We drove up the mountain road and are now stuck. All vehicles have officially been closed to the mountain— Sheriff's orders. He cited dangerous, slick, and treacherous roads. Sadly, there was an accident, too, and it will take hours to clear it all up. That's why the local officials closed it until the snowplows arrived. There are law enforcement, official vehicles, and tow trucks everywhere.

Caitey wrote back: **You can't sneak past—and drive really carefully?!** Her text was written to be more of a joke. She certainly didn't want her parents to get hurt or their vehicle to slide off the mountain.

Mom wrote back: **No, sweetheart. And I'm quite sure your father isn't up to dragging our vehicle off-road and shoveling snow while wearing his best suit.**

She added a smiley emoji, and Caitey knew they were both being playful. But it was so disappointing. Despite video chats every week, she hadn't seen her parents in months.

Hopefully, we can get up there tomorrow, sweetheart! We'll spend the night in Santa Barbara and keep in touch.

Caitey sat down on her bed with a thud. They weren't going to make the wedding. Not. At. All.

She jumped when a final message from her mother came through.

Please give Jenna and Logan our best. We are so happy for them. Take lots of pictures!

Caitey's phone clattered to the carpet. She wanted to cry. The perfect wedding day was turning into ruins. Jenna must be beside herself. She needed to get downstairs pronto.

Quickly, she dressed in jeans and a warm sweater top, then blew out her damp hair with the hair dryer she found in one of the drawers, and then applied her makeup. She was *not* appearing downstairs in the public rooms without blush and lipstick. Not when Jenna's and Logan's mothers were so gorgeous every minute of the day.

Even her own mother, as an ambassador's wife, wore classic dresses and heels, along with getting her hair done every few weeks. There was always some meeting, luncheon, or function to attend.

When a certain Mr. Marcus Stirling roamed the house with those devastating looks and macho chiseled jaw, she had to look as good as possible.

Caitey gave a little shiver just thinking about the guy's shoulders and muscular chest, along with deep brown eyes like melting chocolate. The shivers she always felt when they passed each other were clearly nerves, along with a powerful attraction to such a fine male specimen occupying the same residence as she was.

Marcus often gave her a mysterious smile or caught her eyes across the room or dinner table. Instantly, she was self-conscious and stupidly tongue-tied.

At first, he'd intimidated the heck out of her . . . Well, what girl wouldn't be when some tall, massive man in a dark suit magically appeared out of the woods?

But after learning his tragic story last night, she gazed at Marcus with new eyes. He'd been a Navy SEAL in a combat zone; he'd been dumped by a woman who lied and stole his life savings and inheritance; and he was a devoted friend to Logan and the Hearst family.

Maybe she needed to give him a second chance and stop avoiding him.

Fifteen minutes later, she grabbed the binder with all the wedding plans and ventured downstairs, searching for Jenna.

But she didn't need to go far. Jenna appeared at the foot of the curved staircase and launched herself into Caitey's arms.

"I don't know whether to laugh or cry," she said in a quivery voice.

Caitey hugged her hard. "It's a shock we never expected, but we'll sit down and figure this out. However, can I get breakfast first? For some reason, I'm starving."

"It's the wintry weather. Come with me," Jenna said, pulling her arm toward the kitchen. "Gus has breakfast on the dining room sideboard. Just like in *Downton Abbey*."

Caitey laughed at the eggs, bacon, toasted bagels, fruit, and three different kinds of juice. "Wow, this is amazing. How does the man have time? Especially with the wedding dinner to prep for."

Gus appeared through the swinging double doors, a big smile on his cheerful face. He tapped the side of his head, and the smile turned into a big grin. "The secret is detailed planning. I've been getting ready for this week for two months. Sit down and eat to have energy for the rest of the day. It's going to be a big one!"

"I still have to fit into my wedding dress later today, Mr. Gus," Jenna chided.

"My food is magical. Everything will fit, I promise."

Jenna gave him a saucy look, lifting one eyebrow. "I'm going to hold you to it."

She and Jenna had just finished eating the delicious breakfast when Jenna suddenly let out a soft shriek and ducked under the heavy mahogany table.

Caitey lifted the tablecloth. "*What* are you doing?"

"I hear Logan's voice coming in the back door. He can't see me until the ceremony! It's bad luck."

"Oh, right, yes! The groom can't see the bride! Terrible luck!" As if the snow wasn't bad luck enough! But Caitey didn't say that part out loud. She didn't want Jenna to go full-throttle hysterical.

Jenna hissed, "Think I can crawl out of here and back upstairs without being seen?"

"No," Caitey said matter-of-factly. "They might head down the main hallway while you run up the staircase."

"What do I—"

Caitey cut her off. "Stay under there, and I'll head the guys off."

"Good idea!"

"Now, ssh!"

Caitey jumped and swung back through the kitchen door just as Logan and Marcus entered the mud room to hang up their jackets and take off their boots. Snow fell off every square inch of them.

"Sorry for the mess, Gus," Logan called out.

Gus appeared at the door and waved a meaty hand in dismissal. He was a rotund man with the happiest face Caitey had ever seen, but how did he dice onions and tomatoes with such finesse with those fingers? It was a mystery.

"Snow will melt," the cook said. "And then I will mop. We will soon have lots of muddy shoes once guests begin arriving."

Caitey leaned against the doorjamb between the kitchen and the mud room.

Marcus jerked his head up to look at her while he stepped out of his boots. He gave her a slow, warm smile, and Caitey felt her heart flip-flop inside her chest.

The tingles of fascination roared back while she tried not to stare at the gorgeous man in his jeans and flannel lumberjack shirt.

The top buttons had come undone while he shook the last snow off, and the temptation to press her lips against the skin of his throat was almost more than she could bear.

Biting her lips instead, Caitey averted her eyes despite wanting to stare at his throat.

So far, she'd only seen him in button-down pressed shirts and ties. This was a new look, as if Marcus had become an entirely different man. No stiff security professional with his take-charge veneer any longer—just a sexy-as-heck man that Caitey found herself fantasizing about.

She shook her head to stop the crazy thoughts from torturing her. She was acting like a sixteen-year-old schoolgirl.

"Um," she stammered. "Can I get you all anything? Towels? A heated blanket? You must be freezing."

Logan laughed. "We're sweating bullets from the shoveling. I'm heading upstairs to take a shower. Where's Jenna? I need to talk to her. This blizzard coming out of nowhere is insane."

"Sorry, no can do," Caitey told him, bracing herself for an

argument. "You don't get to see Jenna until she walks down the aisle!" she sang gaily.

Marcus gave a low whistle, followed by a chuckle. "Logan, take it from me. We know the boss around here today is Miss Wedding Planner. In capital letters."

Caitey gave him a sideways glare while trying not to laugh.

Then, her skin sizzled as he gazed at her most curiously. As if he was seeing her in a whole new light. She stared back, trying to sternly flash her eyes, but then she stifled a laugh because he merely grinned as if he knew what she was thinking.

Good grief, what was going on between them? Where had this chemistry come from? Or had it been there all this time while she tried to ignore it and push it away?

"Jenna and I will discuss the snow, any delays, and the change-up of plans. We have a *lot* to talk about. And I'll let you know what you need to do later on."

Stepping toward the door between the kitchen and the dining room, Caitey scanned the place for signs of Jenna. Their dirty breakfast plates still sat on the polished table. "Jenna?" she hissed.

Slowly, the draperies on the far wall next to the windows overlooking the rose garden shifted and rustled. Jenna's head peeked out. "Is the coast clear?"

"Not yet, but I left you under the table, and now you're behind the curtains. Stay there while the guys go upstairs and get showered."

Caitey clamped her mouth shut the moment Logan and Marcus came through the dining room on their way to the foyer and the staircases. "No!" she cried, worried Logan would spy Jenna behind the curtains. "Go through the *other* doors to the drawing room first—"

Marcus raised a finger to his lips and made a shushing noise. "Your secret is safe with me," he said, his words low and sexy as his eyes darted toward the draperies.

The shivers his voice created raced down Caitey's neck like a runaway freight train.

Logan paused at the exit doors that led to the marbled foyer, glancing back over his shoulder. "Will you tell Jenna that we need to talk?"

Jenna's voice came from behind the drapes, muffled as she tried to squelch a giggle. "Caitey and I have it all figured out. Don't worry, Logan. Leave it to the wedding planner."

Her fiancé whipped around, trying to spy out where Jenna was hiding, and then he chuckled and shook his head when he saw the draperies rustling. "You are one silly, adorable woman, Jenna Thornton. I can't recall the last time I hid behind any curtains. Guess there's a first time for everything."

"Caitey and Marcus will take care of everything," Jenna replied, "while I spend the rest of the hours until the ceremony making myself beautiful."

"You couldn't be any more beautiful than you already are, my love," Logan said. "Even when you're hiding behind the curtains. I have to admit that there are days it feels like we're living inside a comedy."

Caitey burst out laughing and then shooed Marcus with her hands, pushing him toward the door along with Logan.

"No peeking and no eavesdropping," she admonished the two men. "It's girl time now. But I do have to ask . . . Did you also shovel the front walks and porch and vestibule in front of the house?"

"Don't worry. We know how to do the job right," Marcus said with a wink of his delicious brown eyes.

Caitey widened her eyes at him, trying to hide the jump in her stomach, then firmly shut the doors behind the two men.

Blowing out breath, she turned to Jenna and lifted an eyebrow. "Okay, my dear cousin. Sit down and let's *talk*, girl."

CHAPTER 15

CAITEY

*J*enna parted the drapes, pushing her hair from her eyes. "What was all *that* about, girlfriend? Did I detect some high-level flirting with one Marcus Stirling, Intelligence Specialist, Navy SEAL dude, and best friend of my groom?"

Caitey flipped her hair over one shoulder and batted her eyelashes. "I have no idea what you're talking about. Right now, I'm pulling out my lists, and we're figuring out your wedding!"

She reached for the binder where she had been keeping all her wedding notes and sat down in one of the high-back chairs.

"I do have a lot of questions—and worries," Jenna said. "I've been trying to hide it, but good grief, I hope my guests can drive up here okay this afternoon. They're probably plowing the road as we speak."

Caitey braced herself and chewed on her lip. "I have fresh intel on that."

"You sound like Marcus," Jenna accused playfully. "I think he's rubbing off on you."

Caitey saluted, laughing at the reference to the Navy SEAL, but moments later, her cousin's eyes filled with fresh tears. "My dream wedding is ruined," she said, her voice quivering.

Caitey grabbed her hand. "No, it's not. We have everything we need to make it beautiful. So first, here's the sad news."

Jenna immediately forgot about herself. "Have you heard from your parents yet? Did they make their flights?"

"Yes, I got a flurry of text messages this morning from my mother. They got in from San Francisco last night and stayed at a hotel because it was so late. This morning, they picked up their rental car. And . . . were stopped at the bottom of the mountain."

"What?! The blizzard was that bad?"

"Yeah, Mom said that the sheriff and deputies are blocking the roads heading up the mountain because it's so icy. And . . . there was a bad accident, so the entire area is filled with emergency vehicles. They had to turn around and ended up getting a hotel room in Santa Barbara."

"That's terrible!" Jenna exclaimed in a faint voice. Then she jerked her chin up. "What about my wedding cake? The bouquet and boutonnieres? They're supposed to be delivered soon."

"Have you looked at your phone for messages?"

Jenna started. "I've been so distracted by the snow . . . and my head whirling about how and where to do the ceremony."

"Where's your phone now?"

Jenna patted her pockets and looked up in a daze. "I have no idea. I must have left it in my bedroom. Let me run and get it."

She jumped up and bounded upstairs, returning in sixty seconds while scrolling wildly through texts and phone calls.

Sinking into her chair again, Jenna blinked back the tears filling her eyes. "The bakery can't deliver. Authorities turned her away. The flower shop as well. And I had an eye-catching and gorgeous bridal bouquet picked out."

Caitey reached out to embrace her cousin, and they held on to each other for a long moment while Caitey tried to figure out how to fix the big mess this day had turned into.

"Guess it's no use crying over spilled milk," Jenna said, her voice shaking. "The wedding isn't going to happen."

"I hate to say this," Caitey said softly. "The closed roads mean your other guests and friends won't be able to attend either."

"You're right! And I wanted to show off my stunning dress!" she added with a wan smile, even though her lips were quivering. The next instant, Jenna's phone rang. She swiped the screen. "Yes," she said solemnly to the person on the other end. "Yes, I understand. Please don't worry yourself. There's nothing to be done. It's just a bad luck day but thank you for calling."

She let the phone clatter to the table's surface. "Well, that's that," she said in a low, tortured voice. She lifted her eyes to gaze at Caitey, her eyes filling with emotion. "The minister marrying us lives farther up the mountain. And he's stuck in his driveway." Her phone buzzed again, and Jenna scanned the message. "Good grief, can this day get any worse? The string trio can't make it, but I should have figured that out already."

"We'll play the 'Wedding March' on the stereo," Caitey told her. "Or Queen! Barry Manilow! The Beach Boys!" she added, trying to elicit a mile from her cousin. "Whatever you want, honey. I think it's obvious that both the ceremony and the wedding dinner will be inside—the ceremony in the drawing room and the dinner right here in this elegant dining room. Gus is on duty and ready to do anything we need. He's truly a dear, isn't he?"

"He is," Jenna agreed in a quiet voice. "Okay, I guess all of that will work, but I'll have to muse on a good Queen track for a while," she added with a trembling smile.

Caitey pressed her hand against hers. "This morning has been a big blow, but *I promise* I will give you the most beautiful and romantic wedding, and you will be filled with joy at marrying the man you adore."

A single tear finally spilled from Jenna's eyes. "But if the minister can't get here, there is no wedding."

Caitey pressed Jenna's hand with hers, leaning in close to

whisper, "Hey, if all else fails we can have Marcus go online and see what it takes to be an officiator for your wedding. Maybe there's an instant certificate he can print out. It means pulling double duty, best man and officiator, but at least you can actually get married, and it'll be legal. And I'll be the wedding planner and D.J. and . . ."

"Thank you for that, Caitey," her cousin said with a wan smile. "I'm so glad you're here. Without you, I'd be a bigger basket case than I already am."

"You know what? I think you should go lie down for the next several hours. Let ME take care of everything down here. I want to create a magical fairyland while you catch up on your sleep so you will look beautiful and radiant to walk down the aisle."

"Really? And leave you with all the work?"

"Don't you worry, I have *lots* of helpers I can recruit."

"Like me," said Mrs. Hearst from the dining room doorway. She strode in with Jenna's mother right behind her.

"I'm not the bride's mother for nothing!" she teased her daughter. "Give me a list, and we'll get it done." She put an arm around Jenna's shoulders. "I'm ordering you back to your room. Sleep, shower, and then I'll be up after lunch to help you dress and do your hair."

Mrs. Hearst leaned in close as if telling a secret. "Did you know that when I was eighteen, I went to beauty school? Although . . . I only did hair and nails for a couple of years before meeting the love of my life. Ever since, Logan's father has been traveling for work and moving around the globe while I trotted after him, having the time of my life going to all the places I'd always dreamed of and jumping into charity work. But . . . I haven't lost my touch!"

Jenna's eyes widened in surprise. "That means—you—"

"Exactly," Mrs. Hearst said with a big smile lighting up her face. "I will do your makeup, hair, and nails today since we can't get down the mountain to the salon. The roads might not be open until tomorrow, if then."

Jenna's jaw dropped, and she let out a small cry. "That means . . . I must cancel our honeymoon suite at the Bed & Breakfast Inn for tonight."

"Nope," Caitey told her. "You aren't doing anything but being the bride today! Logan will cancel it and rebook after the roads are plowed."

"But—but what about tonight?? It's our wedding night! We—we can't stay *here at the house with everyone else . . .*" Jenna's voice trailed off.

Aunt Vicki dropped a kiss on top of her daughter's hair. "Your new mother-in-law and I have already thought about that, and we have a plan!"

Mr. Hearst strolled into the dining room, looking for lunch. He scanned the women's faces when they all turned to look at him with frowns. "Am I in the doghouse? You all look flustered, or angry, or—"

His wife slipped an arm through his. "You do know that the roads are blocked, don't you, dear? This means no wedding guests, flowers, cake, or honeymoon suite."

Her husband's eyes widened. "True, true. It's quite disappointing after all the hard work. I'm so sorry, Jenna. Do you want to reschedule the wedding?"

Jenna shook her head. "All of my vendors *and* the musicians have already canceled the orders. At least, they can't deliver until the roads are cleared—which could take days. We have no idea when we can get off the mountain. But I guess when the cake is delivered you all will be feasting on sugar for a week afterwards while Logan and I are on our honeymoon. And the flowers will scent the house for days— or wilt and fall apart, just like my wedding is . . ."

"Oh, Jenna!" Caitey said, fighting back her own tears at the desperation in Jenna's voice. "This blizzard has socked the mountain like never before. Once in a century freak storm! Time for Plan Two—which we are creating this very moment."

Mrs. Hearst widened her eyes. "It's terrible, but it's our son's wedding day, darling," she told her husband. "We're rallying everyone to pull this off for Logan and Jenna."

"Of course, Isabella—right! Just let me know where I can pitch in," Mr. Hearst said.

"I had an idea," his wife said. "As an attorney and previously on the county board, do you have the legal authority to perform the wedding? The minister is stuck too."

"Good thinking. I'm not sure but let me find out for certain. Oh, what about Caitey's father? I understand he's a United States ambassador. There's a better chance of him being able to perform a wedding ceremony than I am."

Caitey spoke up. "My parents flew in yesterday, but it was

extremely late. They attempted to drive up here this morning but were stopped due to the accidents and the road being closed. We won't see them until the roads are cleared, in a few days."

"That's not good news," Mr. Hearst said.

"I'm sorry my sister and her husband won't be able to make it," Aunt Vicki said. "I spoke with them an hour ago, and they're so disappointed to miss your wedding, Jenna."

"I'm still trying to wrap my head around the fact that this entire day is completely upended and it's already going on noon." Jenna's face turned red while she tried to remain composed in front of everyone.

Caitey piped up. "Jenna, it's time for you to head up to your room and relax while we finish preparing. This wedding will move forward," she added firmly.

"There's the spirit," Mr. Hearst said. "Now I will go into my office and call about marrying you and Logan. Where did he and Marcus go? Haven't seen them in the last few hours since I spied them outside clearing the snow."

Everyone in the dining room glanced at each other as Gus pushed through the swinging doors with a giant tray of sandwiches, chips, dip, and cookies for lunch.

"Time to eat and get that energy back? And pardon me for eavesdropping, Mrs. Hearst, as I was maneuvering this tray of food. Logan and Marcus just finished bringing in the wet chairs from outside after scraping all the walkways."

Caitey grabbed Jenna's arm. "Go hide!" Then she grabbed a paper plate, loaded it up and shoved it at her cousin. "Take this upstairs before Logan sees you. Eat, take a nap, and then shower. Show time is in five hours!"

"Five hours!" Jenna squeaked. "You're crazy!"

Caitey gave her a secret smile. "Just you watch me. But first, follow me!"

She took Jenna's hand and moved toward the doors that opened into the beautiful marble foyer. She did some quick reconnaissance and spotted Logan striding back outside to get another load of chairs.

"Hurry upstairs now! Before he sees you!"

"Ay, ay, Captain Caitey!" Jenna saluted, then climbed the stairs as fast as she could.

After her bedroom door shut, Caitey waited to see Marcus come back inside the house from the rear gardens. Only Logan returned with the last couple of black cushioned chairs. He took a towel and wiped them down, then finished arranging them in rows.

"Where's Marcus?" she asked with an innocent tone. "Wasn't he helping you just now?"

"Yeah, of course. He, um, had to take off for a while," Logan said vaguely. "But the chairs look good here in the drawing room. We'll have Reginald build a roaring fire, and it'll be nice and warm. Now, I'll set up the arbor for the ceremony—right after I bring a load of firewood inside."

"Well . . ." Caitey drawled slowly, wondering where in the world Marcus would have. The man was an enigma. A phantom at times.

"Yeah?" Logan said, turning toward her with a smile.

"Oh, um," Caitey promptly said. "I'm just rethinking the arbor. It will look so plain and empty without the flowers that were supposed to be here."

"Maybe my mother has some garland and ribbons from her stash of Christmas decorations."

Caitey gave him a wan smile with a brief nod. Jenna did not want a Christmas theme. She wanted autumn with splashes of color, fresh but elegant sprays of flowers, and ribbon and tulle in warm golds and browns.

While Logan returned to the back door to retrieve the aforementioned Christmas decorations, Caitey sighed. Somehow, she had to pull this thing off. She promised Jenna that it would be spectacular. There was nothing to do but haul all the boxes of wedding decorations she'd brought with her that were stored in Mrs. Hearst's study and start decorating.

After she ate a quick sandwich. Because her stomach was growling obnoxiously.

But mostly, she was left wondering and perplexed about where Marcus Stirling had gotten himself off to. She needed both him and Logan to help her hang and pin.

Maybe he was doing his twice daily rounds of security camera checks.

But with all the multiple feet of snow that had fallen, *nobody* would be lurking about the Hearst mansion today.

But where did he watch the live feed to see if any potential property breaches were filmed on those cameras? Was he in some secret room in the house? In an office in one of the garages?

She was silly to think about that man. Or was her reckless heart betraying her senses? Every time she was near him, Caitey thought she might swoon. Like a character from a gothic romance.

Too many questions to ponder now. She had a wedding to get ready for—pronto!

CHAPTER 16

MARCUS

The gardens were shoveled and swept of snow, as were the front porches and open-air vestibule that graced the entrance of the Hearst mansion before the imposing double front doors.

He'd helped Logan dry the chairs, and they'd set them up for the ceremony. In the dining room, he could hear Caitey, Jenna, both mothers, and Mr. Hearst talking.

Jenna slipped past, bounding for her room. At least Logan hadn't spotted her when he dropped a load of firewood into a box by the fireplace.

When Jenna spied Marcus, her eyes grew large and panicky. She motioned to Marcus to stay quiet, then put a hand to her throat and sliced across it in a simulated fatal gesture. She didn't want him blurting out her name, so Logan spun around to see her.

Her soft footsteps turned into tiptoes while the bride disappeared to the second floor, and Marcus kept her secret.

Marcus desperately wanted a shower, but he refrained for now. He had two more errands to run. Secret errands. He left a note for Logan and hauled on his coat, hat, heavy gloves, and boots—thankful he'd packed a pair of long johns, too.

He had a trip down the mountain to make and a deadline of only five hours.

He couldn't wait to see Caitey's face upon his return.

CHAPTER 17

CAITEY

*C*aitey stood back to admire her handiwork.

The elegant cylinder glass tubes sat along the entire aisle of the chairs. She was glad Logan and Marcus had placed the arched arbor in front of the fireplace. Guests could come in the front door—if they had any actual guests—and be quickly seated with a beautiful view of the drawing room.

Maggie had polished the grand piano. Reginald had jumped in to vacuum the luxurious carpets on the elegant and expansive parquet floor.

After lunch, she had talked with Gus about food. That man was prepared for anything—a disaster, an outbreak of the flu, a run on the grocery stores—he was ready.

Caitey could smell the sweet and warm aroma of the wedding cake Gus had just taken out of the oven. Three perfectly baked layers. And now he was creating his special homemade frosting. When he'd shown Caitey his past decorating photos, she knew he was a master at just about everything in the kitchen.

The cake was going to be magnificent.

Since two deep freezers were in the large pantry, he'd pulled out fifteen filet mignon steaks when he heard about the caterer being stuck in Santa Barbara. He planned to create a beautiful spinach salad with all the trimmings and some hot vegetable dishes topped off by his famous homemade dinner rolls.

Caity unwrapped the boxes filled with tall red and white candles and began placing them inside the glass cylinders. She would light them just before the ceremony began.

She still had the linens to place on the backs of the chairs and the yards and yards of ribbon she'd brought.

She added a centerpiece on top of a lace drapery on the grand piano.

Then Mrs. Hearst showed her how to use their in-house stereo system. Everything was digital, and the massive music collection was set up so she could choose a song with the press of a button. All she needed to know was Jenna's choice, although she had selected a few love songs to play as guests were arriving.

She needed to stop thinking about "guests" arriving. Nobody was going to make it up the mountain by dusk, that was for sure. Maybe she should have set it up for fewer people, so it didn't look so empty when the ceremony was performed.

Maggie had been keeping Caitey abreast of the roads, the weather, and the police reports on the radio. At this point, it was just family. So, even with the household staff, there were only about eleven of them. A small, cozy group, she had assured Jenna—who she hoped was still resting!

Time continued to march on. It was almost time to shower and get dressed herself!

Reginald entered the drawing room and set the fireplace with a stack of neat, cut logs. He selected a long match and rested it against the hearth for lighting.

Caitey stared at the arbor, wishing she had brought more decorations now that they had no fresh flowers. But she had to stop berating herself. Nobody had a clue there was going to be a blizzard this week!

Just then, she heard a door open and then slam shut. Mr. Hearst took the stairs quickly, heading straight toward Caitey when he reached the bottom.

"Has something happened?" she asked.

"I have been on the phone with my secretary and some other attorneys in the area." He paused and gazed at Caitey pensively. "The sad news is that I can *not* perform Logan and Jenna's wedding. Attorneys don't have the credentials and are not endowed with any authorization. Any judge may do so, but all the judges I know live an hour away. And with the roads . . ."

"That means the wedding is truly off?" Caitey whispered, almost afraid to speak the words out loud.

Mr. Hearst slowly nodded. "We just have to wait for the road to get plowed and salted. Perhaps in a few more days. I hope you're available to stick around, Caitey?" he asked.

"Of course! I promised Jenna she would have her beautiful, wished-for wedding. I kept hoping . . ."

"I, as well. Those two have been waiting a long time."

"Well," Caitey said, trying to maintain her composure. "We'll eat Gus's beautiful dinner, light the fire, and play charades?"

"Unless Jenna is weeping in her room," Aunt Vicki said, overhearing their conversation as she entered the drawing room. "My poor daughter, it's practically got me in tears, too. What horrible luck. Of all the years to have a blizzard in early November!"

"How is Jenna doing?"

"I checked on her a few minutes ago, and she's still resting," Caitey's aunt said with a small smile. "I didn't want to disturb her, but I'll make sure she's up and showering in about thirty minutes. I know she wanted to get her hair done all fancy in town, too, and that has gone by the wayside. But thankfully Isabella has offered to help Jenna with her hair and makeup. Until you're in the middle of a wedding, one has no idea of the hundreds of details until things begin falling apart!"

"That's for sure," Caitey said.

"How fortunate that her new mother-in-law has experience with all of that. I always tell myself that everything works out in the end. She'll be happier once she and Logan can always be together. He steadies her, which is funny because Jenna has always possessed a calm personality. She runs her busy, busy Coffee Loft shop with such skill. Never frantic. Always smiling and polite and unhurried for her customers."

"Did we ever hear about her friends, Marina and Wade Kennedy? They were supposed to fly in from New Orleans."

"Just before she laid down for a nap, she got a call from Marina. Their flight arrived fine, but they're also stuck in town, barely snagging one of the last hotel rooms."

"By the way, have you seen Marcus Stirling around?" Caitey asked nonchalantly. "I was hoping he might help me move some furniture," she added lamely.

"Alex and Mr. Hearst can do it for you, although the room looks wonderful already. When the candles are lit, the room will be magical."

Her aunt glanced at the grandfather clock. "Oh, my, it's time to start showering and dressing! I will see you in an hour, sweetheart."

She hugged Caitey and hurried up the curving staircase.

Caitey watched her disappear upstairs, and fatigue hit her like a brick wall. She inched her way over to a small loveseat pushed against the far wall and plopped down.

One by one, she ticked off her To Do list. This was the moment she hated. The fear of forgetting something!

The downstairs was quiet. She assumed Mr. Hearst was in his study, but perhaps he had already gone upstairs, too.

Gus was whistling from behind the kitchen doors. Maggie was upstairs, making sure Jenna had everything she needed.

And . . . Mrs. Hearst was most likely assembling her beauty tools and makeup palettes to help the bride.

It was time for Caitey to start dressing, but she didn't need nearly as much time as Jenna. She was still going through the motions as if the wedding would occur. But the dirty little secret was the fact that there was *no* wedding. There couldn't be because there was nobody to marry them!

Hot tears pricked Caitey's eyes, thinking about Jenna upstairs. Was she bawling her eyes out?

Caitey moved to the surround-sound stereo system and selected Christina Perri's romantic song, "A Thousand Years."

Instantly, those tender, gorgeous lyrics floated all around her, and she stood in the center of the drawing room, closing her eyes while daydreaming of romance and finding her true love.

If Jenna and Logan didn't get married today, it *would* feel like a thousand years waiting for each other. Her own love story was as far away as the moon. Pluto, or beyond! A tear of frustration rolled down her face at what a disaster this day had turned out to be.

Just as the chorus began, the front doors opened and closed with a bang. Startled, Caitey jerked her head up.

Freezing air swirled inside, crawling up her legs while goosebumps broke out.

Heavy footsteps crossed the marble foyer, halting at the drawing room doors. *Who could that be?*

Just when she was about to call out, Marcus appeared in the doorway, taking off his shoes so that he didn't muddy the carpet.

He wore so many layers of clothing that he looked like a round snowman.

"Marcus?!" she spluttered. "Where did you come from?"

"The North Pole, I think." He burst out laughing. "It is bitter out there!"

His face was red, and there were traces of snow crystals on his cheeks, including a pile of snow covering his knit hat.

"Why are you wearing so many layers? Earlier, you just had a jacket and gloves on while shoveling snow. You *went* somewhere, didn't you?" Caitey accused in a muffled voice.

Her brain was trying to catch up with the sight of this man. He was so rugged and handsome, even with snow sticking all over his body and a red nose from the freezing temperatures.

Marcus gave an embarrassed laugh. "You caught me. I went on an expedition."

Caitey stared at him even harder, moving closer as if he had become an electromagnet drawing her in like a force field bringing in the mother ship. "That's . . . very mysterious. Have you been out in the wilds hiking? Are you a cross-country skier or a wilderness wild man who exiles himself from civilization?"

He chuckled, and Caitey bit her lips when she realized that she was flirting with him! No, she wasn't supposed to like this guy! The man who pierced her with his gaze and followed her around the room with his warm, chocolate eyes.

"Miss Caitey Belgrave," he said softly. "I have a surprise for you."

"A surprise?" she burst out. "For me?" she added with a squeak. Now she was chirping like a bird, but she was also trying to rein in her emotions before he saw that she had been crying at today's disaster, at the romantic love song, at everything that had gone so wrong . . .

Marcus had caught her off guard, that was for sure.

"Are you okay, Caitey? Has something happened while I've been gone?"

"What hasn't gone wrong?" she said, trembling. "I wanted to give Jenna her dream wedding, but we no longer have a minister. He's stuck up the mountain and can't get out of his house."

Marcus's eyebrows shot up. "You mean Logan's father isn't authorized to do it?"

"No," she whispered, blowing out a shaky breath.

"Hey, hey," Marcus said softly, moving toward her. His face was gentle, and his eyes filled with concern as he tugged the knit hat off his head, revealing a thatch of disheveled hair that Caity was so very tempted to touch.

Before she knew it, she and Marcus stood only a foot apart while he stroked a finger across her cheek. "You've either been out in a rainstorm, or that was a tear I detected."

"Oh, yeah, I *wish* it was just a thunderstorm," she whispered. She was frozen, gazing at him, the bristle on his cheeks that needed shaving, his beautiful eyes looking deep into hers. The touch of his finger tenderly touching her face . . . and now his hand was cupping her cheek.

Caitey sucked in a breath and wavered on her feet. "You're pretty good at detecting," she added, trying to lighten the intense moment. Why was she *this close* to launching herself into his arms? She wanted someone to hold her and comfort her after the day's stress. And she couldn't think of anyone else she wanted, only this guy. This *man*. Marcus Stirling: Protector, Master of Security, professional at making her feel seen and cared for, especially after too many thoughtless past boyfriends.

All at once, his face broke into a smile. "Stay right where you are," he commanded. "Don't move."

"What? Why?"

"Because I have a surprise for you," he said.

"A surprise? I'm not sure I want any more surprises today. I'm ready for a nap. And, well, I'm kind of mad at you right now."

"Mad at me? Why?"

"Because you've been gone for *hours*, and I needed help. I couldn't find you . . ."

That wasn't exactly true. He and Logan had set up the

arbor. Both mothers had been helping Jenna with hair, makeup, and dressing. Gus had made the cake and was now frosting it. She'd found the perfect song, but the day had been incredibly stressful, and the wedding hadn't even started yet.

Marcus reached out to lightly touch Caitey's arm. "Today has been incredibly stressful for you—for Jenna—for everyone. You're doing a remarkable job coming up with ideas and contingency plans. I think—I actually think you're pretty amazing."

Tears smarted Caitey's eyes at the compliment. "Wow, thank you, Marcus," she whispered.

"But right now I have something I'm dying to show you outside. So *do not move a muscle*," Marcus added with a wink.

Caitey shook her head at him, holding back the bubble in her throat. "I promise I won't! But what are you up to? More shenanigans?"

"The *best* shenanigans of the day!" he announced, throwing open the double front doors. "Now close your eyes, or it won't be a surprise!"

A blast of frigid air swept through like a cyclone. She heard Marcus step out onto the expansive entryway and return almost instantly with a cart filled with plastic bags. He halted in the doorway to the drawing room.

"What have you done?" Caitey asked softly, tempted to slit her eyelids open to see what he was doing. Right now, she was so confused that she had no idea what was happening. "The staff is going to kill you for bringing in mud and snow onto these marble floors."

"No worries because I'm the clean-up crew." Marcus tugged off his thick gloves, then held out his hand, grasping hers in a warm, firm grip.

The adrenaline rush and attraction toward him was like a fifty-foot wave, knocking Caitey's senses in a thousand different directions. Her hand in his was perfection. Those fingers, the power and warmth that emanated from him, were unlike anything she'd ever experienced.

She wasn't sure she'd ever had this strong feeling with any other man, just from *holding his hand*!

When she wavered, Marcus softly said, "Trust me, Caitey, my girl. You are going to love this."

He'd called her *my girl*. Was that just a tease, or did it mean something more? Could he possibly feel the same explosions of chemistry between them as she was feeling?

"What are in those bags?" she finally asked.

She moved to his side as he opened the tops of each large plastic bag in the cart. Inside were flowers—bundles upon bundles of flowers—like a flower garden, bouquet after bouquet, had just sprung up from the earth below and erupted like a volcano in the mansion's foyer.

"This is the same bridal spray that was ordered for Jenna!" she whispered, reaching out to touch the exquisite bouquet. "And these are the boutonnieres for the men. Oh, my! These bunches of roses, lilacs, and daffodils are to decorate the arbor! And the aisle and the candles and . . . everything!"

Caitey's legs gave out from the shock. She was about to sink to the floor when Marcus put both arms around her, holding her tightly against him, his face close, his breath warm and sweet, his strength so powerful . . . "I think I might faint with shock," she whispered.

"Go right ahead, I've got you," he said softly.

"I don't understand how you got all the flowers I ordered from the flower shop. What did you do—break in and rob it? This is like a dream!"

"I'd love to make all your dreams come true, Miss Caitey, wedding planner."

"Now you're shamelessly flirting, Mr. Stirling."

"If I'm not mistaken, you're holding on to me as tightly as I'm holding you."

"Cheeky man!" she teased.

"I'm claiming the first dance with you, and we can dance cheek to cheek in real-time," he teased. "Just like that song, 'Dancin' Cheek to Cheek' when Fred Astaire sings it to Ginger Rogers."

She pulled back and stared at him, a smile quivering her lips. "How do you know old songs like that?"

"My grandparents helped raise me while my mom worked full-time. We watched a lot of old movies. So, how about it? Can I sign your dance card?"

She shrugged. "I'll save the first slot for you, but the rest of it I can't promise. So many men are here; you might have to fight them all off."

"You're not wrong there. I know of two fathers, Gus and Reginald, the minister, and I'm sure after the bride and groom get done, we'll all be dancing together."

Caitey burst into laughter. "I suppose my dance card really will be filled up. You'll have to meet me behind the couch later."

"Hey, I like the sound of that."

Caitey halted. She pressed a palm against Marcus's broad chest. Whoa, his muscles were more defined and sculpted than she expected . . . "Wait a minute. What did you say? How would the minister's name be on my dance card?"

Instead of answering her question, Marcus asked, "Has Logan returned?"

"Returned?" she echoed. "I didn't know he'd been gone, too. I haven't seen him for quite a while. I've been a little busy. You still haven't answered my question about the flower shop . . ."

"Oh, yes, I got distracted . . . you do distract me, Caitey," he said quietly. "Ever since you caught me coming out of the woods."

She shivered at the compliment *and* the atmosphere pulsing between them. Vibes she had tried to ignore ever since she had arrived at the Hearst Estate.

She smiled softly at the compliments he was showering on her, but she couldn't let him distract her any longer. "I still have one big question, Mr. Stirling. *How in the world* did you get past the closed roads?"

A mischievous smile lit up his entire face. "Easy-peasy. All I did was get my snowshoes and winter gear on and hike down to the mountain village. It was only three miles. If I'd had to go to Santa Barbara, I'd be walking until midnight," he chuckled. "I called the florist and told her I was coming. Verified by Jenna's mother so the florist would have them ready and let me hike back up the mountain with them."

"You must be exhausted!"

"I've done much more strenuous things than this. Besides, it was for a worthy cause. As best man, I have my duties, you know."

"Oh, gosh, *you—this is so amazing*," Caitey choked, emotion overwhelming her. "Thank you."

"The show must go on," Marcus whispered, leaning in to press his lips against the top of her hair.

Caitey froze in place, wanting the moment to go on a little longer, but Logan appeared at the dining room doorway, another gentleman in tow. "Hey, Caitey and Marcus," he boomed out, happiness lighting up his face. "Allow me to introduce Reverend Cecil Callaghan. He's the man we've all been waiting for. I think we're having a wedding after all!"

A burst of laughter escaped Caitey's throat. "Okay, this is too much. *Where* did you find a minister at the last minute?"

"He lives three miles *up* the mountain. I hiked in one direction while Marcus went in the other. Just in time, too.

The magic hour is fast approaching. I'm going upstairs to shower and get my tux on!"

"May I help with anything?" Reverand Callaghan said with a slight Scottish accent. "I've known the Hearst family for many years and have been looking forward to Logan and Jenna's nuptials. We met together a few weeks ago. The snow was quite a surprise this morning. I called Logan and asked if he'd help me through the snow-piled roads. He got his snow-mobile out, fetched me, and here we are."

"That's absolutely *perfect*," Caitey said with a sigh. She turned to Marcus. "Thanks to you and Logan, we *are* having a wedding!"

CHAPTER 18

MARCUS

*A*fter taking off his heavy coat and hat then picking up his boots from the front door and putting them away, Marcus watched Caitey move about the room, finishing the last touches on the arbor now filled with the fresh colorful fall flowers.

She was good at this, and she had a special knack for all the details. For example, she wound the gold, red, and mauve k ribbon and tied the flowers so that the petals and blooms fell precisely right.

Last, they lit the tall, slender candles with long matches until the entire room glowed a soft yellow. The aura of romance was breathtaking. And right in the middle of it, Caitey smiled and bounced with delight.

She was in her element. Marcus wanted to gather her in his arms and twirl her around the room. He wanted to know what she felt like in his arms. What it might be like to kiss those beautiful, luscious lips finally.

Inwardly, he groaned with attraction to her. It was a strange sensation after so many years . . . to finally meet a woman he wanted to get to know better—a woman who made him *feel* again. Hope again. And perhaps, if she felt the same way, to finally look forward to the future instead of just going through the motions of life. Working, surviving, but not truly living.

When she was finished twirling around the piano with delight at her handiwork, he slipped his hand into hers.

"I have a surprise for you," he said softly.

"A surprise? For me? You've already surprised me so much today. You were the answer to my prayers that somehow a miracle would happen, and Jenna and Logan would have their wedding." She lifted her eyes to his, and he saw the shiver run through her sexy body. "Um, right now, we both need to go get dressed. And I need to tell Jenna everything is ready! Oh, where did the reverend get to?"

"I think he's in the study with Mr. Hearst. But quit changing the subject, you charming, beautiful woman."

"Who, me? Don't tease me, please. Don't lie to make me feel better."

"Hey, I'm an Eagle Scout, and I do not lie. Nor do I say something to a woman without meaning it. But . . . it's not something I've said for an exceptionally long time, and only to one other woman in my life."

"What?!" she burst out.

167

Marcus watched Caitey blink in astonishment at his words as if she wasn't quite able to accept that his compliments and attraction for her were not only rare but true feelings.

"I—I," she stammered, as if working up her courage. "I'm sorry," she finally said. "Jenna told me a little bit about . . . what happened to you a few years ago. It's horrible and must have been so very painful."

Marcus was glad Caitey already knew so that he didn't have to go through the humiliating details, but he had to say something to assure her. To let her know that the event was so far in the past, it had no hold on him any longer.

"Once I got that sock in the gut on the morning of our wedding and learned Shelley's true motivations, I knew I had been lied to about everything. For years. Shameless, cruel lies. She purposely set me up in the worst possible way. Any love I thought I had for her quickly turned to hate."

CHAPTER 19

CAITEY

*I*mpulsively, Caitey reached for his arm in a gesture of sympathy and comfort, then pulled back, but Marcus didn't let her stop. He grasped her hand and lifted it to kiss the back of it, tenderly smiling the entire time while his eyes fastened on hers.

Caitey's legs trembled. Wow, this man was romantic. Was he for real? Nothing like this had ever happened to her.

"I don't want to talk about that liar and swindler or think about her ever again. Instead, I have a surprise for you."

"A surprise?" she echoed. "You've already given me the best surprise of my life! I'm still reeling in shock . . ." Not to mention the feeling of his warm skin along her fingers, the moment they had just shared, his generosity in saving the wedding . . .

"Come with me." Marcus grasped her fingers in his, laced them with his own, and led her into the shadowy kitchen.

"It's kind of dark in here," Caitey said. "Where's Gus?"

"I came in the back door before I surprised you at the front. Gus is taking a break before dinner. But everything is ready, as you can see."

Caitey peeked at the wedding cake displayed in all its glory on the large worktable. It was frosted and—

"You brought the flowers I needed for the cake, too!"

The beautiful glass wedding topper had been affixed, and the gorgeous wedding cake was ready for serving.

"Smells good in here," Marcus murmured, studying the interior of the fridge while Caitey looked over his shoulder.

All the salads were prepped and ready for serving. The filet mignon beef was marinating on the kitchen counter and ready for grilling. A chocolate fountain was prepped and ready to be plugged in for melting—several types of fruit were sliced and wrapped in plastic to hold under the chocolate fountain waterfall.

"Wow, these rolls smell amazing!" Caitey exclaimed, glancing under the towel of a large bowl stacked with fluffy homemade rolls.

Even the dining room table had already been laid with fancy wedding china, gold-rimmed water goblets, real silver cutlery, and champagne chilling on ice.

"Gus has been mighty busy," she said with a small laugh.

"Yeah, he's pretty amazing."

"What time is it?" Caity asked, whirling about to find the

clock on the wall reading four-thirty. "I need to get upstairs to Jenna and see what else she needs before the wedding march begins!"

Marcus grasped her hand and led her to the table. "You need five minutes off your feet and a snack to fortify your strength. I'll bet you never ate lunch today."

"Oh, I had a quick one, compliments of Gus, the most amazing man with endless energy. "But when I get engrossed in my work, the hours fly by, sometimes too fast."

"When you love what you do, that's the best part. When it's time for camera checks, the hours whiz by," he said, giving her a sly sideways glance. "It even makes me act a little weird and stalker-like when a beautiful woman comes into my binoculars' view."

Caitey gave him a playful slap on the arm. "You're incorrigible, Mr. Stirling."

"Yep, that I am!" he agreed. "Right now, sit down while I reveal my surprise."

She gave him a quizzical look. "I can't imagine what you're talking about . . ."

Marcus picked up a tightly secured brown bag with a logo and set it down on the kitchen table. Then he sat beside her, pulling up a chair. "We still have a long time until dinner, so while I was in the village picking up flowers, I brought you this."

He opened the bag and reached in to pull out a Lofty-sized Coffee Loft Styrofoam cup. When he pulled off the lid, steam curled up from the hot cocoa.

"It used to be piled high with whipped cream, mini marshmallows, and shaved bits of chocolate, but they already melted."

"You *didn't*," Caity whispered in shock. "You brought me a gift! My favorite!"

"And . . . ta-da, one for me," he added with a laugh. "Enjoy a few minutes off your feet."

"Oh, *yum*," Caitey murmured when she took the first sip. "The Coffee Loft makes the best hot cocoa ever. Jenna says they have a secret recipe."

The room went quiet momentarily while they sipped their cocoa and gazed at each other. Caitey tried not to feel self-conscious every time Marcus caught her eyes and gave that sly, sexy smile of his.

But oh, my, the man was sending alarm bells of attraction over every square inch of her skin, from her head to her toes.

"Hey," he said after a moment, "I'm not sure I ever heard if your parents made it here."

"They're in a hotel in Santa Barbara. They tried to drive up this morning, but of course, they were turned away. I hope the road will be plowed by tomorrow so they can visit."

Caitey saw genuine concern in Marcus's eyes. "It must be strange not to have them here."

"It is, especially when my father flew across the Atlantic for Jenna's wedding. I haven't seen them in over a year, not since two summers ago when I went to Portugal and spent two weeks sightseeing and shopping with my mom. At least

I'm here with Jenna, my Aunt Vicki, and Uncle Alex." She paused and stared down into her cocoa.

"Is your Coffee Loft cocoa speaking to you?" Marcus teased, reaching out to lift her chin so she would look at him. "Or maybe it's those disappearing miniature marshmallows calling your name . . ."

Caitey laughed, swatting at his arm. "This sounds weird, but maybe it is . . . something has been nagging at my brain all day, and I can't figure out what I forgot." She jerked her head up when her brain clicked into gear. "The photographer! I never heard from him! We won't have any pictures of the wedding! This is terrible!"

She ran into the dining room, where she had left her phone while decorating, and scrolled through emails, texts, and voicemails.

When she looked up again, Marcus was at her shoulder. "Any news?"

"Yes, he did call a few hours ago and left a message that he couldn't get up the mountain. He lives in Santa Barbara and comes highly recommended."

"You may not know this, Caitey, but I'm an amateur photographer. I've taken a few classes and have a good camera from my SEAL days. I'll take the photos while the rest of you enjoy the ceremony."

Caitey's voice broke with emotion as she impulsively threw her arms around his neck. "You're saving the day once more, Marcus Stirling, security man," she said softly against his cheek. Wow, he even smelled good—all citrus musk with an outdoor scent from hiking through the forest roads.

Flustered, she brought her arms down. "Sorry for the exuberance," she muttered, her face burning.

"Hey, I was hoping I might get a little closer to you," he whispered, not letting her drop her hands all the way but sliding his own warm hands up along her arms to bring her closer.

Then Marcus wrapped his muscled arms around her waist and lifted her a few inches off the floor while she buried her face into his shoulder. The smell of flannel and sexy man was about to make her swoon.

"You're strong," she whispered into his ear jokingly.

"Nope, you're light as a feather."

"Um, you'd better let me down now; I hear Maggie and Gus and Reginald coming in through their wing of the house."

Marcus gave a low growl, not wanting her to pull away. "Can't let them catch us in a comprising position, can we?"

Caitey's toes slipped to the floor while he kept her arms around his neck. "We are *not* in a comprising position. I was thanking you."

"Don't let that stop you. I'll need some more gratitude later tonight."

"Cheeky SEAL," she retorted, smothering another surge of laughter.

When Gus and the rest of the staff entered the kitchen,

Caitey was busy clearing away the hot cocoa while Marcus headed upstairs to shower and change.

"Everything looks beautiful and delicious," Caitey told Gus.

"I aim to please," the cook said. "I had help from Maggie here, and Reginald has been taking care of the dining room and running upstairs for the rest of the family who need various items, like extra towels."

"I'm off to shower and dress myself now," Caitey said. "See you in thirty for the ceremony. Well, maybe forty-five minutes!" she added with a laugh.

First, she was going to check on the bride! Knocking quietly at Jenna's door, Aunt Vicki immediately opened it and rushed Caitey inside. "Come look at our bride!"

Jenna stood in the center of the suite, moving in circles in front of two full-length mirrors. Mrs. Hearst clapped her hands together in delight. "You look stunning, my dear," she said softly, kissing Jenna on the cheek and then holding both of Jenna's hands in hers. "My husband and I could not be happier that this day has finally come. Logan loves you to pieces, and you are a splendid couple."

"Thank you, Mrs. Hearst," Jenna whispered, smiling repeatedly at the sight in the mirrors.

"How many times must I ask you to call me Isabella, sweetheart? Mrs. Hearst is so formal. Especially after this crazy week of blizzards and having to develop a Plan B, C, and D to pull this off."

Caitey took Jenna's hands in hers. "You look smashing, woman!"

"I love my dress even more today than when I purchased it," Jenna said. Her figure suited the mermaid style with its half-train, lace, and heart-shaped bodice.

"Your hair is perfection!" Caitey said. "Wow, Mrs. Hearst, you certainly know what you're doing. And your makeup is stunning, Jenna. You're like a *Vogue* model."

"And you are too funny, Caitey," Jenna said.

Caitey shook her head. "Nope, you're a princess about to marry her Prince Charming!"

"Is it true we have a minister here to perform the ceremony?" Jenna asked, still disbelieving.

"I met him myself," Caitey told her, smiling. "He even has a terrific Scottish accent. He's been hanging out with the fathers for the last hour or two. Your groom picked him up at his house on a snowmobile and brought him down himself."

"Seriously?" Jenna said, clapping a hand over her mouth. "Logan is amazing. He saved the day! A few hours ago, I thought we would have to postpone it all. But there's only one thing that still worries me."

"What's that?" Caitey asked. "We can *make it happen!*"

"*Where* are we going to spend tonight? Our wedding night? We can't get to our hotel!"

Mrs. Hearst and Aunt Vicki exchanged secret smiles.

"We consulted our genie bottle," Aunt Vicki told her daughter, "And Isabella showed us a special guest suite on the third floor. While you showered and dressed, we were up there with Maggie preparing it for the newlyweds. You'll have the entire floor to yourselves. And a privacy door to the stairs that lead up to it."

Jenna's mouth dropped open in shock, and her eyes filled with tears. "Everything is turning out perfect. Thank you, everyone, for pulling this off for me and Logan."

"Isn't it wonderful—" Caitey began.

Before she could finish her thought, the power in the mansion went out, and Jenna's bedroom suite plunged into darkness.

CHAPTER 20

CAITEY

Caitey froze in place, the bedroom blacker than midnight. Jenna, Aunt Vicki, and Mrs. Hearst gasped in unison as if from the shock of the inky darkness.

In the next moment, she could see the faint outline of the window glass and a slow fringe of the winter moon creeping like molasses from the horizon. A few stars dotted the deep black sky.

She felt, rather than saw, Jenna crumple to the floor, her wedding gown spooling around her. "The power went out! Why does this day keep getting worse?"

Outside the bedroom door, sudden footsteps pounded on the stairs—not from *up* the circular staircases but coming down from above them.

Maggie appeared with a glowing lantern in one hand. "Is

everyone okay? Jenna, sweetheart! So sorry, love. On the happiest, most anticipated day of your life, too."

"Where did you come from so fast?" Mrs. Hearst asked, glancing backward into the pitch-black hallway.

"I was up in the honeymoon suite, ma'am, putting the final touches to the room before the ceremony begins. What a pity about the power! But I already have a plan!"

"Candles!" Caitey burst out. "And lanterns! Oh, Jenna, you will have the most romantic wedding of the decade!"

"Oh, I agree!" Aunt Vicki said. "That *is* romantic."

"But do we have enough candles and lanterns, Maggie?" Mrs. Hearst asked.

"Yes, ma'am! I always stock extra in the fall since we get a power outage or two during winter. I texted Gus, asking him to bring several boxes upstairs for the bedrooms, along with lighters and matches. And then we'll go downstairs and place candles all over the drawing room, hallway, and dining room!"

Caitey hurried over to Jenna and embraced her, brushing away the day's disappointment. She *had* to step in and *be* the wedding planner! "It's going to be so unique and lovely! A wedding you'll never forget! Think of the stories you can tell your children!"

Her cousin stuck a hand on her hip. "Let's not get ahead of ourselves, dear Caitey! I'm still trying to get through today! Gosh, I've had to rewire my brain's expectations over and over again. But candles *will* be quite lovely, too," she admitted. "Hey, Mom, can we sneak a peek at the honeymoon suite?"

"Of course, Maggie did a gorgeous job!" Aunt Vicki exclaimed. "But then we need to get downstairs for *the wedding* before your groom and the fathers start wondering where we are."

"True! And I'm too excited to wait any longer."

Caitey followed her cousin up to the third floor of the mansion. There were only a couple of suites and a closed-up storage area that Jenna said led to an attic.

Jenna swung the doors wide open and halted at the entrance.

Caitey gaped, dropping her jaw. This room was the most dramatic in the entire house.

Candles of every size and color sat on antique tables and dressers. The carpet was soft and plush, and the roof pitched into a peak with chandeliers hanging from the center over a luxurious king-sized poster bed.

"Of course, the chandeliers will have to wait until the power comes back on, but they are so pretty!"

The draperies that fell from the scrolled wooden slats were a pretty shade of maroon and edged in silver. A pile of plump pillows sat on top of an exquisitely embroidered bedspread.

"Come look at this bathroom," Jenna said next, tugging at Caitey's hand. "It's even better with all the lights. But the shower is huge, and there's a bathtub deep enough to sit in with bubbles."

"I noticed the fireplace in the bedroom, too. That will be useful tonight since the house is without power; we no longer have any heaters running without power. I can feel a chill starting."

"I feel it, too," Jenna admitted. "Maybe I need to ask Reginald to light the fireplace now."

"I'll get him on it. Now go freshen your makeup and spritz your hair while I go downstairs and start the entrance music." Caitey slapped a hand to her mouth. "No! I can't begin the music for your bridal entrance with no power to run the stereo and speaker system!"

Jenna's face began to crumple again. "The bad news never ends . . ."

Caitey rushed forward. "Please don't cry. Not today. It's been a super stressful, horrible, no-good day, and I wanted everything to be so perfect for you—"

"That's not your fault," Jenna interjected, wiping her eyes. "I'm just weepy about all of it. Everything I dreamed of for today has been turned upside down—or worse!"

Instead of giving in to the panic she'd been experiencing all day, Caitey squared her shoulders, hugged Jenna tight for a moment, then gazed into her face. "The *most* important part of this wedding is that you are marrying the good man you love. You get to spend the rest of your life with wonderful, kind, handsome Logan Hearst. We'll look back on all this craziness and laugh—and we'll think it was the coolest wedding ever!"

Jenna's lips quirked up a little. "Cool as in blizzard conditions, that's for sure!"

Caitey laughed. "I will figure something out! Come down in fifteen minutes," she ordered. "This wedding is on schedule—well, kind of," she laughed. "And in case I forgot, Marcus is your substitute photographer!"

"Wow, Caitey, you think of everything! But you still need to get dressed, too!"

"Good grief, I forgot to get into my bridesmaid dress! Up until the snowstorm, I was the backup bridesmaid. Marina is supposed to be here standing next to you."

"Since I love my cousin, you are the perfect replacement. Get moving, girl!"

Racing back to her bedroom, Caitey heard the murmur of voices as the dads, the groom, the minister, and the mansion staff gathered in the drawing room.

Stopping in her tracks, a new worry exploded in her mind. "How in the world is Gus going to cook the filet mignon?"

Once in her room, she hurried through a second shower after the day's decorating and worry, the scent of gorgeous Marcus lingering on her skin. This entire weekend had been a series of unexpected and furious events.

After dressing, Maggie knocked on the suite door to tell her to meet Mrs. Hearst, who was waiting to do her face and hair in Jenna's room.

The elegant bridesmaid gown was a sweeping satin burgundy shade with lace accents. She twirled in front of the full-length mirror, loving how it looked on her.

Two minutes later, Mrs. Hearst got to work on her hair. Soon, she had a chignon hairstyle, sparkly earrings, and a necklace set with delicate ringlets hanging from her face.

Caitey twirled in front of the mirrors while the older women clapped their hands. "Thanks for making me look like a princess next to Queen Jenna!"

"You look lovely, Caitey," Aunt Vicki said softly, squeezing her hand. The entire main floor was suffused with the glow of hundreds of candles when they descended the staircase. Maggie *was* a miracle worker!

"It's absolutely beautiful, but I'm worried about the music and the dinner meal—how will it finish getting cooked and baked?"

Mrs. Hearst brushed a nonchalant hand through the air. "I'm very blessed with great staff. Gus got the generators going—he had already stocked the propane tanks for the winter season, thank goodness. The oven is doing the last baking, and the gas grills are grilling," she added with a little laugh. "Our wedding dinner will be delicious."

"That means we also have—" Caitey began to say.

"Yep," a male voice said, striding out of the shadows.

Marcus was incredibly sexy and masculine, towering under the foyer chandelier with his broad shoulders in a deep gray suit as best man. "Let's go start the music, Miss Caitey."

Her heart skipped a beat. She didn't think any man could look *so* dang good. Those shoulders, that chin, that mouth, those deep, melty hot cocoa eyes with a side of rich Godiva chocolate!

"Um—um—yes, let's start the music," she stammered as he came forward and took her hand in his firm, warm fingers to guide her into the drawing room toward the built-in stereo system. In moments, Pachelbel's "Canon" was playing softly in surround sound, filling each downstairs room and floating up the elegant staircases.

Marcus turned toward Caitey and gazed at her, lifting her hand to kiss the back like a 19th-century gentleman. "You are a vision, Caitey," he said in a deep voice. "Perfection."

"You're looking mighty fine yourself, Mr. Stirling," she said, her chin lifting. "I didn't know you cleaned up so well."

A grin spread over his face, and his eyes crinkled at her teasing. "Hey, I'll take whatever you give me."

Caitey tapped a finger against her lips. "I do have one final question for you, Mr. Stirling."

"What's that, lovely Caitey?"

"If you're standing with Logan as best man, how can you possibly take pictures, too?"

"I'm one step ahead of you. I showed Reginald how to work my camera, and he'll be snapping all evening. At least through the ceremony."

"You think of everything," she said, batting her eyelashes.

"I aim to please," he said, his lips curving into a smile.

"The bride is at the top of the stairs!" Aunt Vicki

announced excitedly. "Come in and take your seats, everyone. No—choose your seats but remain standing for the wedding procession."

"Oh! I must get up there to come *back down* as the bridesmaid!" Caitey slipped her hand from Marcus's grasp, picked up the skirts of her gown, and ran up the staircase. Jenna stood waiting at the top, gnawing at her lips while Caitey's jaw dropped. "You look *so* gorgeous, Jenna," she hissed. "Truly, your dress is magnificent. Definitely made just for you!"

"A far cry from my stained apron at the Coffee Loft, right?" Jenna quipped.

"Stop chewing on your mouth; your lipstick is coming off and will stain your teeth!" Caitey giggled.

"Is it too late to back out?" Jenna suddenly said in a low, panicked voice. "Terror just hit me right in the gut!"

Caitey held both her hands in her own. "Cold feet are normal. This is the moment it hits you. The magnitude of what's about to happen. You're becoming Mrs. Logan Hearst for the rest of your life, from this night forward—"

Jenna's eyes grew wider with panic.

"Okay, I'm shutting up now." Caitey squeezed her hand. "Girl, you *want* to marry that man, Mr. Logan Hearst. You will have the best honeymoon, live happily ever after, and have beautiful, perfect children. This is a wedding to remember, and we'll all be telling stories for years to come. Don't let a few jitters get to you."

"What would I have done without you, Caitey?"

"You would have eloped. But now we all get to see your ceremony, and we get to eat Gus's fantastic food and that cake—wowza, we'll each have three pieces . . ."

Jenna finally grinned and gave a relieved little laugh. "I'm so glad you're my wedding planner. You always make me laugh. I confess I wanted perfection, but life doesn't work like that. But Logan *is* perfection. And I love him with my whole soul."

"Whew! Glad we got that out of the way!" Caitey said, teasing her. "Then I think we're gonna have us a wedding ceremony right now, girl! Follow me! If you fall on these stairs, I'll be here to catch you."

At that moment, the music downstairs swelled, and Caitey began to descend, followed by Jenna a few steps behind.

The music was soothing and beautiful while Caitey took one slow step at a time.

When she arrived at the doors to the drawing room, she gasped in sheer delight. The beautiful flowers scenting the air, and the magnificent glowing candles had created a fairy tale.

Caitey tried to remain demure as she approached the aisle between the two rows of chairs, where everyone stood with huge smiles on their faces, watching the small procession.

The music swelled a little louder as Jenna stood in her gorgeous white gown in the doorway. She looked like a queen with her thick blonde hair piled beautifully on her head while diamond teardrop earrings dangled against her neck. Her bridal bouquet, filled with blood-red orchids and lilies, was stunning.

Bless that exasperating and delicious Marcus Stirling!

CHAPTER 21

CAITEY

*I*nstinctively, as soon as Caitey thought of him, her eyes darted toward where he was standing next to Logan in front of the minister.

He was already gazing at her with that beguiling smile of his. That man had disarmed her over the past few days. He had become her knight in shining armor, saving this wedding single-handedly.

She mouthed, "Thank you" to him as she passed, and his grin grew wider while one eyebrow lifted in a sexy expression. Even after the wedding was over, she felt the night would not end until much later.

Caitey's stomach jumped into her throat. Good grief, these peculiar feelings for Logan's best man were so unexpected after their first encounter two days ago that she didn't know quite what to make of them.

Even so, the tingles running up and down her skin were *real.*

Standing on the opposite side of Jenna and Logan as the minister began the proceedings was a bit surreal. Caitey couldn't stop herself from repeatedly catching Marcus's eyes —it was hard not to when those deep chocolate pools were directly in her line of sight!

A slow grin crossed his lips as if Marcus could read her mind. He smiled gently and slightly nodded, showing her that he was gazing at her just as much.

Caitey forced her eyes toward Reverend Callaghan after he had spoken a few words of marital advice and began the official ceremony.

"Do you, Logan Hearst, take Jenna Thornton to be your lawfully wedded wife? To have and to hold from this day forward, in health and sickness, for richer, for poorer, for as long as you both shall live?"

"I do," came Logan's strong reply as he lifted his hand to kiss the back of Jenna's hand. "For the rest of my life and beyond," he added in a low voice.

Soft laughter followed. Then the minister turned to Jenna asking her the same questions, and Caitey noticed her cousin's eyes brimming with happy tears. When she said, "I do," she and Logan immediately kissed and embraced each other.

Then Logan dipped her downward, kissed her again like a hero from an old movie, and gently raised her up again while the room exploded with clapping and laughter.

Marcus scrambled to the stereo panel, and the triumphant "Wedding March" began. Everyone began chattering and congratulating the newlyweds.

After a few minutes, Marcus lifted a hand and said, "Before we sit down to the wedding dinner, we'll have the bride and groom's first dance as husband and wife. Following that, a few minutes of dancing for anyone ready to kick up their heels."

"Or kick *off* their heels," Caity muttered before realizing the room had quieted for a split second. The entire group heard the murmured remark and burst into laughter.

Reginald appeared in the doorway. "Ladies and gentlemen, the wedding dinner will be served in fifteen minutes in the dining room. The place settings are marked with each guest's names."

"Thank you, Reginald," Charles Hearst told him. "The bride and groom dance first, please. Logan, please escort your new wife to the dance floor."

The music changed again, and the lovely sounds of Christina Perri's voice floated over the room while she sang, "I have loved you for a thousand years . . . I'll love you for a thousand more."

After a few moments, Marcus was at Caitey's side. He leaned into her, touching the back of her hand with his. "You're looking a little melancholy, Caitey girl. You okay?"

"Oh, yes, I'm fine! I just . . . get a bit emotional at weddings, especially when it's people I love so much. And this song . . . it's perfect, Marcus. It's an excellent choice for this evening. It's one of those songs where you dream about that one person you'll love for a thousand years ... forever."

"And is that why you became a wedding planner?" Marcus asked softly.

"It's because I was a disaster at everything else," Caitey said with a touch of laughter.

"I doubt that."

She glanced up at him and coyly batted her eyelashes in sarcasm. "You do not know the half of it, buddy. I've been fired from so many jobs. At least now I can work for myself —even if I have to rely on a lot of vendors to come through —but I can pick, choose, and charge what I want. Although I'm still paying off student loan debt."

"Where'd you attend?"

"UC San Diego, of course, my hometown college."

"I remember at dinner your first night, you saying that you'd majored in business and interior decorating. Sounds like the perfect combo for a wedding planner. You did a wonderful job here—before and since your arrival at the intimidating Hearst Estate. It's not an easy feat to come into a place like this. I certainly didn't grow up like this, even though I spent a lot of my childhood here with Logan."

"Well, thank you for that. My early life was modest until Dad went into politics a few years ago and became an ambassador. His ancestors are from Portugal, so he worked that angle to get the position. He even speaks Portuguese."

Marcus lifted his eyebrows. "You do have a more

European look about you. You must be giving off vibes. Will you tell me sometime about those other 'jobs'?"

"Maybe," she said, giving him a sassy smile.

"Before this beautiful love song ends, will you please do me the honor of this dance, Miss Caitey Belgrave?"

"Oh!" She hadn't expected that question! And yet, he *had* asked her for the first dance yesterday.

"We are the only people here *not* dancing," he added slyly.

Caitey didn't need prompting or the extra motivation. She wondered what being in Marcus Stirling's arms would be like. That broad chest was asking her to come closer . . . if she was honest with herself, she'd been wondering for two days now. Ever since sitting at the Coffee Loft with him that first day. Despite her nerves. And the mysterious woman in the photograph.

Jenna's story about Marcus's past made him vulnerable and deserving of sympathy, just like everyone else. For all his confidence, good looks, and natural charm, he wasn't immune to bad relationships. Or heartbreaks.

Just like her dating experiences, which always ended badly, or the guy just disappearing into the ether after one or two dates.

Before she could nod, Marcus had stepped in closer to take her in his arms, swaying gently in time with the music. This Navy man knew how to dance! Who could have predicted that?

Their hands fit perfectly together, and the moment she was in his arms, his other hand slipped around her waist with a firm, protective grip. In high heels, Caitey could look into his face. She never remembered dancing being this personal, this romantic.

Being so close was a little intoxicating, and she stumbled slightly at the decisive moment of his presence. He held her tighter, and the stumble was barely a bobble as if he'd anticipated it, and within seconds they were in sync.

The song swirled around her, enclosing her with this man like one beat, one heart. *". . . all along, I believed I would find you . . . Time has brought your heart to me . . . I have loved you for a thousand years . . . I'll love you for a thousand more."*

The dinner gong sounded, and the chatter crescendoed as everyone worked their way into the dining room and sat at the table.

When the group entered the dining room for dinner, dripping red candles created a second fairytale castle experience. The food was beautiful, and the atmosphere was one of joy, smiles, and laughter.

Caitey had been placed across the table from Marcus. They could gaze at one another but not speak very easily when they had dinner partners on either side who kept talking to them.

Dinner became a blur of each course, with food so delicious it melted in your mouth: homemade rolls dripping with butter, rare filets that sliced smoothly, asparagus tips, a spinach raspberry salad with vinaigrette dressing, and finally, the most delicious wedding cake.

Jenna and Logan fed each other cake and champagne, and

the easy chatter and laughing were so lovely after all of Caitey's worries the past few days.

Caitey ate the last bite of her cake and set down her fork when she spied Logan and Jenna, beginning to make their move towards the stairs leading to the honeymoon suite.

Her cousin leaned in as she passed, hugging her. "Thank you for the best wedding ever, Caitey. I hope the snow begins melting tomorrow so you can get home . . . but of course, you can stay as long as you want."

"I hope you make your flight to the Caribbean where your private island awaits!" Caitey told her. "It's been a beautiful day. Congratulations again to you and Logan. May you live happily ever after as you experience all the ups and downs of your beautiful life together."

Jenna and Logan disappeared through the doors, and all Caitey could hear was the swish of her wedding gown in the marble foyer.

She rose from the table, and Marcus caught her eye. He said, "Meet me back there," lifting his chin to indicate a quiet corner of the dining room.

Caitey practically did a double take at the surprising request. The thought of meeting up with Marcus for a private conversation shot a case of butterflies straight up her stomach and into her throat. Sizzles ran down her neck, and those flying butterflies were going crazy.

What was that all about?

CHAPTER 22

CAITEY

A minute later, when she moved toward him, Marcus was grinning like a teenager. "I think we're letting all that snow go to waste."

Caitey laughed. "How does snow go to waste?"

"There are mountains of it, and nobody wants to go out and play. How about you and me? We'll make a snowman. Snow angels. Walk under the moonlight."

"Wow, Mr. Navy SEAL Man, you appear to have some romantic bones underneath that dinner jacket. But alas, I didn't bring any snow clothing. I was wearing a short-sleeved dress two days ago."

Aunt Vicki passed by, overhearing the conversation, and giving them both a knowing smile. "You can borrow mine, dear. I'll go get it and bring it to your room."

Shaking her head, Caitey added, "It must be going on eight o'clock and already dark outside."

A mischievous grin spread across the man's lips. "That means we'll have all the snow to ourselves."

Caitey shook her head, stifling a giggle. "You are too funny, Mr. Stirling. But I'm game."

Actually, the idea of going out into the dark, under the night sky, alone with him after a house full of people, sent shivers of anticipation down her neck.

Minutes later, she was bundled up and tromping outside in snow boots, a scarf around her neck, and gloves on her hands. "Wow, look at those stars!"

"Pretty great, huh? Up here on the mountain, there are no city lights to dim the sky, although if you squint your eyes enough, you can see a faint haze where the mountain village lies that connects to the highway into Santa Barbara."

"The village where the Coffee Loft is, right?"

"I have memories of that place," Marcus said softly.

"Hm. I do too. . . certain secrets were about to be revealed."

"No secrets anymore. It's all a bad dream from so long ago, and I never think about it anymore. And especially when I'm with a beautiful woman," he added meaningfully.

"Will any beautiful woman do for your purposes?"

He let out a laugh. "That was tart."

"Sorry, I couldn't help myself."

"I can tell," Marcus said, turning to gaze at her while they paused for a moment to plow their boots through a snow drift. "I must admit that ever since I met you, I haven't thought about anybody else."

Caitey's breath caught. Was he serious or just flirting?

He soberly added, as if reading her thoughts, "I'm not just complimenting you to flirt. I'm serious. I never expected these last few days with you."

Marcus paused to take her hands in his, gazing at her full in the face. "I love your eyes, tentative smiles, gorgeous thick hair, and funny personality."

Caitey was so caught off guard by his compliments that she didn't know what to say. Instead, she lifted her chin to the inky black sky filled with so many stars it was like a tube of glitter had spilled to create the Milky Way. "It's a full moon, too. So beautiful. As if I could reach out and touch it," she added in awe.

"Shall I lasso the moon for you?" Marcus asked.

Caitey gazed up into his face while the soft sound of snow shushed beneath her boots. "*It's a Wonderful Life,* right? When George lassos the moon for Mary."

Marcus stopped in his tracks. "I have never known any girl to get that little joke of mine."

Caitey stuck a hand on one hip. "How often have you used it on other women, sir?"

"Um, actually, none," he admitted. "I've spent most of my adult life overseas in hot climates, hunting bad guys."

She pressed a hand on his arm, knowing all at once the difficult things he'd experienced over the past decade serving in the armed forces overseas. Including the heartache and embarrassment of being taken for everything. Not just his savings but his heart. "Does it haunt you very much?" she asked quietly.

"No, not much. At first, it does, but you learn to categorize the elements of war: the terrible fear, the death, the suffering of innocents. We were taught to place it in a mental lockbox with our dirty socks and worn-out boots. We had to survive. To make it back to the real world without going insane."

Before Caitey could move her hand away, Marcus reached out to take her gloved hand in his while they trudged through the snow until they came to an empty clearing in the woods a little higher than the Estate house. Soft, glowing candlelight created splashes of gold in every window.

"It's simply beautiful," Caitey sighed. "What a magical day. And to think this place terrified me when I first arrived."

Marcus gave her a sideways grin. "You were sure I was a madman or a stalker."

"No, I didn't . . . oh, look, it's starting to snow again!"

"Are you changing the subject?"

"Who me? Never."

Tiny snowflakes fell softly around them, then larger, fluffy ones that sparkled under the dimming light of dusk. The sky blended deep purples and soft blues, and the world fell quiet as the snowfall muffled every sound.

"Shall we make snow angels?" Caitey asked, her heart

pounding against her ribs at his closeness and the talk of personal matters.

Marcus chuckled. "Thought you'd never ask."

Seconds later, they were both lying on mounds of soft, new snow and waving their arms and legs to create wings.

"I haven't done this since I was a kid," she confessed, laughing at the overhead view of the sky filled with a million sparkling gems while her cheeks grew colder by the minute.

Marcus's dark hair was dusted with snow, and his rich, brown eyes gleamed with mischief. But now, looking at her, something else flickered in his gaze—something more profound that looked like he'd been fighting for a long time.

Caitey's cheeks flushed, and her lips parted when she caught her breath. Her arms slowed their angel wing movements, and her hair tumbled from beneath her hat.

Marcus rolled over in the snow, watching her, close and personal.

Despite the cold, the heat between them was undeniable. Their emotions and attraction were palpable, as if the air buzzed with so many unspoken words.

He reached out, his gloved hand brushing snow from her shoulder. Caitey felt a shiver—not from the cold but from his closeness. His nearness thudded at her heart, beating so hard she feared it would fly out of her chest.

She met his eyes, wide and dark, her breath visible in the chilly air. Her lips trembled with emotion, and attraction swelled inside her. Fighting against the close, personal moment of the magical night.

Marcus appeared to hesitate as if fighting against the same feelings and holding on to that last shred of control before slowly, inevitably, leaning in close.

The world shrank around them, the snow, dusk, and cold fading away when he traced a finger down her cheek, gazing into her eyes. His breath was warm, his lips hovering just a whisper away.

Caitey's pulse quickened, a thrill racing up her spine as the distance between them disappeared.

When Marcus closed the last few inches between them, his warm, soft lips met hers, soft at first, tentative, as though both were testing the waters, feeling the weight of what they'd been avoiding. But then the kiss deepened, the restraint between them snapping as Caitey fully met his kiss, her arms going around his neck.

His hand cupped her jaw, his thumb brushing her cheek, sending heat coursing through her despite the freezing air around them.

It was intoxicating—the way his lips moved against hers, both gentle and urgent, as if he'd been starving for this, for her. Every sensation was heightened—the way his breath hitched, the snow falling around them like a silent witness. Her heart pounded, but all she could focus on was the feel of him, the taste of him.

After several long moments, Caitey tried not to swoon from the sheer power of his mouth tasting her, kissing her over and over again.

"You are enchanting," he said in a low, husky voice. "It's like I'm living a dream."

"No more nightmares," she whispered while they lay there breathless.

The world around them slowly came back into focus, the snow, the cold, the twilight—but everything had changed.

"I feel like I've just been given a second chance at life," he told her softly, his fingers lifting the curls of her hair around his finger.

"Not all weddings are a horrible disaster," she said quietly.

He gathered her closer, his warm cheek against her icy cold one. "I've been getting a strong premonition," he murmured into her ear, "that *this* wedding is going to lead to a very big change in my life."

Caitey gave him a soft smile as her hands brushed against the rugged, faint bristle of a day-old beard. "I suggest we celebrate with—"

"Another kiss," he interjected, leaning down to press his lips against her neck.

"Well, that, of course," Caitey admitted with a little laugh, her throat tingling with the delicious feel of his lips on her skin.

She wanted to laugh and then cry with delight at this incredibly romantic and handsome man. He was offering himself to her. *To her,* of all the women in the world this devastatingly fascinating man could choose from. "And, since I can't feel my legs or feet any longer, I propose—"

His eyes lit up. "Yes?"

"Hot chocolate—pronto! I'm a master at making hot cocoa. I have many memories of sitting up late at night with my mother, talking and drinking hot cocoa. After Jenna bought her Coffee Loft franchise, she taught me more about how the Coffee Loft creates their unique, divine taste."

"Shall we shake on it?"

"Nope, I can't feel my fingers or toes any longer, but you can carry me back to the house," she said with a wicked grin.

"Thought you'd never ask," he chuckled.

Marcus helped her to her feet, then effortlessly picked her up and trudged through the snow back to the estate's lights.

"You do this amazing well, Mr. Stirling," she whispered, holding her frozen cheek against his while he walked.

"I did a tour during the winter season in Afghanistan. This snow is baby-level powder, nothing like those rugged mountains with multiple layers of ice underneath five feet of snow to trip a guy up. I had to carry about a hundred pounds of gear and weapons, so *you* feel as light as a feather."

"That's very romantic," she quipped. "But hopefully, I'm a little lighter than gear and guns."

"Absolutely, Caitey girl," he said with a chuckle.

It was fun to make him laugh, and moments later, they entered the house through the back doors leading to the kitchen. The clock on the wall read just before midnight.

The place was empty, quiet, and clean. Not a speck of

after-dinner dishes or pots and pans. Gus was thorough and spotless.

Nobody was in sight, even as Caitey held on to the back of Marcus's coat while he peeked into the dark dining room and then the dusky drawing room. The wedding flowers still scented the air, but they were the only people still up at this hour.

Only a few dim night lights remained burning in the foyer, which would help them find their way to the staircase when they finally turned in for the night.

Back in the kitchen, Caitey found mugs and spoons. Chocolate chunks to crush while she filled a copper kettle with milk and lit the stove.

While waiting for the milk to boil, she raided the pantry for marshmallows and checked the fridge for cream.

"Aha!" she crowed softly. "Whipped cream in a bowl. I think Gus had a hunch. He told me that he keeps the pantry stocked with great hot cocoa fixings."

When she laid everything on the table, she caught Marcus gazing at her, arms folded onto the table while his eyes followed her around the room.

"You're making me nervous!" she accused as she held a hot pad over the kettle's lid to keep it from spilling while pouring the heated milk into their mugs. Almost instantly, the chocolate chunks melted into the hot milk. "Stir," she commanded.

Sinking into her seat next to him, they stared at each other while mixing the milk and dark chocolate.

"Now the marshmallows," Caity said, dropping a mix of miniature and large fluffy white pieces onto the hot creamy milk. "And last but not least, the whipped cream!" she said dramatically, picking up a spoon to take a big scoop from the bowl and drop it on top of the steaming cocoa.

Immediately, the extra ingredients began to overflow.

"That's our cue to *drink fast!*" she said, slurping at the edge of the mug and proceeding to burn the top of her lip. "Oh—ouch!" Hurriedly, she set down her mug while Marcus silently laughed at her antics.

"Let me blow on yours to cool it. I think my whipped cream already cooled mine," he told her.

Caitey gazed into his face while he cooled her drink—careful not to cause any whipped cream to go flying—then took a simultaneous sip while gazing at one another.

They set down the super-sized mugs without speaking and leaned in for a kiss.

The chocolate taste on Marcus's lips, combined with sweet cream, was sexy and intoxicating.

"Right now, I think I have everything I've always wanted," Marcus said in a deep voice. He placed his hand against the back of Caitey's head and tugged her closer while she slowly slid out of her seat to cuddle in his lap.

"I'm living inside a dream," she murmured against his mouth. "This is so unreal and yet so magical. I never want to go back to real life."

"The truth about magic is creating it one step at a time."

"So, which step are we in?"

"Hmm," he mused, giving her a sly smile. "Was it the first moment we saw each other, or was it the fantastic kisses in the snow, or is it drinking hot cocoa with whipped cream mustaches?"

"Are you saying I have a mustache?!" Caitey blurted out with a little cry of horror.

"Just a tiny one right there." He leaned in and kissed it off her upper lip. "There are endless steps to the magic of love and life. And we create it every single day. Will you be my magic?"

"Oh, yes," Caity whispered. "But first, you must promise to help me un-decorate this house and load up my car. Then I'll know you really mean it."

A burst of laughter came from Marcus's throat. "I never know what you'll say next, but I can do that. I can do anything. As long as you never accuse me of being a stalker ever again."

"From now on, I'll wave into the hidden cameras and pretend you're my Prince Charming when you suddenly appear out of thin air watching me with your binoculars."

"I think we can arrange that, sweetheart. Besides, those binoculars are magic ones. I see lots of beautiful things through them, especially one certain woman."

Caitey shivered when he spoke the endearment. "I never thought our first encounter at the Coffee Loft in the village would end like this. It's a little surreal."

"It is, but you captivated me from the moment I first saw

you driving in crazy circles around the house, trying to find a live person at home."

"I was not driving in circles! And I'm never crazy."

"Everyone is a little crazy. But you are a ridiculously cute crazy. I think I'll keep you."

"And I think I'll keep you, stalker dude. On one condition," she said in a flirtatious tone.

He leaned in closer to grin at her. "Name it. Anything for you."

"As long as *I'm* the only woman you see in your secret, hidden cameras. For the rest of our lives."

ALL THE COFFEE LOFT FALL
SEASON ROMANCES!

Click HERE to READ this Entire Popular Rom-Com Series!

Welcome back to The Coffee Loft!
A new round of stories has been brewed

especially for you.

Those of you stopping by to visit again, we've missed you. The feeling of home is the same that you loved before. If it's your first time, prepare to be swept off your feet.

While our menu hasn't changed, we think you'll be pleased with the fall favorites we've added. Fans of pumpkin-spiced lattes, peppermint mochas, and rich, chocolaty cocoas will not be disappointed. This multi-author collection of stand-alone sweet romcoms is filled to the brim with the swoons you love and adore.

From sweet kisses to grand gestures and matchmaking surprises, each mug and story will be filled with everything you crave. So come on in and let us serve you with that happy ever after you've come to expect

To shop the full Fall Coffee Loft Collection: https://books. bookfunnel.com/thecoffeeloftseriesfallcollection

LET'S KEEP IN TOUCH!

When you subscribe to Kimberley's Reader Club, you'll receive the small-town Romance, WHEN WE DANCE as a Welcome Gift!

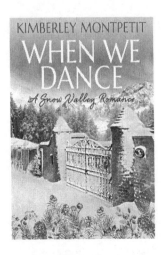

SUBSCRIBE AT THE FOLLOWING LINK for Newsletters

packed full of Book News, Freebies, Book Sales, Audiobook Promo Codes & More!

Click
Here to Join Kimberley Montpetit's Newsletter for Lovers of Romance!

ALSO BY KIMBERLEY MONTPETIT

Read Kimberley's Heart-pounding Romantic Suspense Series -
Danger, Humor, Suspense, and tons of swoony romance!

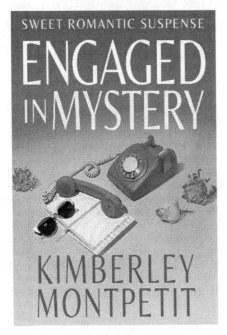

BOOK ONE

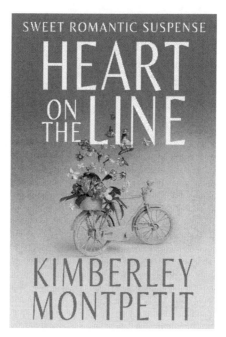

BOOK TWO

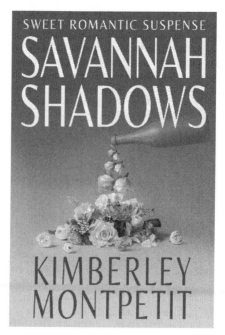

BOOK THREE

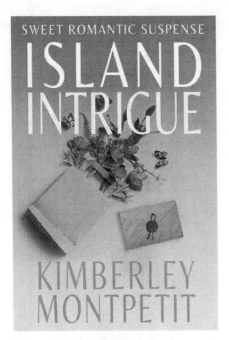

BOOK FOUR

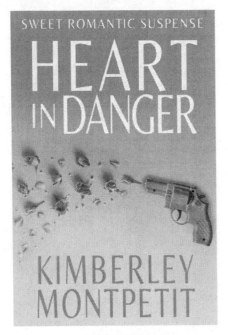

BOOK FIVE

A romantic & bestselling series set in small-town Snow Valley:

WHEN WE DANCE

SPARKS IN MONTANA

BRIDGING THE DISTANCE

UNBREAK MY HEART

THE ROAD TO US

Complete Collection: *Love in Snow Valley*

A Secret Billionaire Romance series!

The Neighbor's Secret

The Executive's Secret

The Mafia's Secret

The Owner's Secret

The Secret Christmas Hideaway

The Fiancé's Secret

A Secret Billionaire Romance Collection - All 6 Titles

The FBI Bride

The Undercover Bridesmaid

An Undercover Bridesmaid Collection!

Mostly Dangerous: The Women of Ambrose Estate

Mostly Perilous: The Women of Ambrose Estate

The Women of Ambrose Estate Collection

FBI/CIA Romantic Suspense Fake Fiance Series

See all of Kimberley's Romance Novels HERE

Subscribe to Kimberley's Newsletter and get free books and the chance for other goodies!

Click Here to Join Kimberley Montpetit's Newsletter for Lovers of Romance!

DEAR ROMANCE LOVER

~

I hope you enjoyed reading *Snow is Falling, Cocoa is Calling!* I love writing sweet romance with action and intrigue that sweeps me into new and wonderful worlds. Please check out my other romance novels on Amazon, including my *Secret Billionaire Romances.* They're all FREE on Kindle Unlimited, too.

If you'd like to be the first to hear about new releases, sales, giveaways, and fun news, please sign up to my Reader's Club Newsletter and never miss a thing. Subscribe and receive a free book! Click Here to Join My Newsletter for Lovers of Romance!

xo,

~Kimberley Montpetit

P.S. Keep turning the pages to read the first chapter in THE NEIGHBOR'S SECRET and THE UNDERCOVER BRIDESMAID from my *Secret Billionaire Romance* series!

ABOUT THE AUTHOR

∽

Kimberley Montpetit once spent all her souvenir money at the *La Patisserie* shops when she was in Paris—on the arm of her adorable husband. The author grew up in San Francisco, but currently lives in a small town along the Rio Grande with her big, messy family.

Kimberley reads a book a day and loves to travel. She's stayed in the haunted tower room at Borthwick Castle in Scotland, sailed the Seine in Paris, ridden a camel among the glorious cliffs of Petra, shopped the maze of the Grand Bazaar in Istanbul, and spent the night in an old Communist hotel in Bulgaria.

Find all of Kimberley's Novels on Amazon

Get FREE Books when you subscribe to Kimberley's Click Here to Join Kimberley Montpetit's Newsletter for Lovers of Romance!

SNEAK PEEK: THE UNDERCOVER BRIDESMAID

Chloe Romano's office line rang while she was wolfing down a chocolate-frosted donut and pouring herself an ice-filled glass of Diet Coke.

The fizzing soda melting over the ice cubes was a sound made in heaven—especially when she was overbooked and underpaid. Which described most days.

Scratch that. *Every* day.

"Can we finish this conversation later, Mom?" she said, leaving the First Lady's office while her mother pored over the details of a fundraising party scheduled in a few weeks. The governor's mansion cook had brought brunch, including the homemade donuts. Mrs. Harvey knew Chloe's favorites were the pastries that boasted at least a thousand calories each. Which she should apply directly to her hips.

"Come back when you're finished, darling," Diana

Romano said. "This paperwork for the Romanian orphanage has to be done by tomorrow."

Orphanages and adoptions—anything to do with children—were the First Lady's passion and life's work, and Chloe often pitched in to help with fundraisers or visits to the children's hospital.

In an attempt to grab the still-ringing telephone, she dashed across the floor to the tiny anteroom. It was originally a closet. Just big enough to hold a small desk and chair.

When Chloe was at the governor's mansion, she had her calls forwarded from her apartment to this office. She kept her cell phone line private, only giving out the number for clients under contract.

"Breakfast of champions," she murmured in ecstasy as she downed the last bite of chocolate.

Chloe managed not to fall into a sugar coma when she snatched up the landline and darted a quick glance at the caller ID, which read Mercedes Romano.

Mercedes Romano? Why in the world would *she* be calling? She hadn't spoken to her cousin since Grandpapa Tony's funeral almost a year ago.

The days of family reunions petered out when all the cousins reached adulthood and spread across the Eastern seaboard. Instead, they relied on the month of August for family reunions and indulging in their former teenage pastimes of sunbathing at Myrtle Beach while eating cherry snow cones and boy-watching.

Growing nostalgic for a real vacation, Chloe quickly said, "Undercover Bridesmaid, Chloe Romano speaking."

"Chloe, is that you?" Mercedes's voice came through ever-so-slightly British and cultured.

"The one and only." Chloe swallowed a gulp of her soda and grabbed for a napkin.

Even though her father was in his second term as the governor of South Carolina, Mercedes had a knack for making Chloe feel like she was wearing overalls and chewing on a wad of tobacco.

"This is Mercedes, your cousin," she said, as if putting on airs.

Chloe laughed. "You're the only person I know with perfect diction and a slight English accent, even though you're not British."

"I did an internship in London for my MBA," Mercedes retorted.

Chloe suppressed a smile. "Blame my despicable lack of memory. So, how are you? To what do I owe this unexpected phone call?"

"Is this new business of yours genuine? Do you really hire yourself out as a bridesmaid?"

"Sounds crazy, but yep, I actually do."

"People pay you money to walk down the aisle, carry a bouquet, and hold up the bride's train?"

"That's part of Package A," Chloe replied, wondering if Mercedes was trying to demean her job, or if she had some other motive. "But it's nowhere near as simplistic as you infer. Sometimes I have to hold the dress up for the bride to use the restroom five minutes before curtain call."

Mercedes let out a sudden laugh. "Spare me the gory details, but enlighten me on what else you do."

"Is your request purely curiosity?" Chloe asked. "Or is this out-of-the-blue call an invitation to hang out with you at the beach this weekend? Because I could definitely pencil you in for that."

Despite her cousin's businesslike tone, she gave a small snort. "Don't be so suspicious, but a day at the beach does sound heavenly. I've hardly slept for a week. My wedding is becoming downright evil to navigate."

Typing on her laptop, Chloe logged on to her website to catch up on the latest email from the various brides she was currently managing. She had a secure interface so they could send email to one another that nobody else could access— like overly curious mothers of the bride, fiancés, or snooping "best friends."

"I understand more than you know," Chloe empathized. "One week out, and most of my brides are ready to bag the whole thing and elope. Or bag the groom and go on a cruise by themselves."

Mercedes gave a light tinkling laugh. "You're so funny, Chloe. I'm honestly curious about your chosen career. After flunking out of your FBI training at Quantico—"

"—I did not flunk out," Chloe cut her off. "I graduated, became an official agent, and then resigned after a year. End of story. If you bring up *anything* about that—so help me I will wring your pretty little neck with my bare hands."

"Wow. Chloe. Okay. Back off, sweetie."

"I'm sure you know the entire story from your mother," Chloe added, a swell of emotion rising in her throat. The memories of her best friend Jenna dying in the FBI house raid often caught her off guard. Clenching her fist, she willed herself not to break down on the phone.

Mercedes went silent for a moment as if she knew she'd pushed Chloe's buttons. "Don't mention my mother. She's driving me up a wall."

Chloe perused her messages, trying to multitask. No bridal meltdowns today. "In what way?"

"Isn't it obvious? I'm supposed to get married in a week."

It was a good thing Mercedes couldn't see Chloe's face. She had completely forgotten that her cousin's wedding was coming up so soon. At the moment, she was swamped with five other brides and *their* wedding to-do lists.

Quickly checking her calendar, she saw that, yes indeed, she and her parents and older brother Carter had tickets to fly up to D.C. for the jolly event.

"So, um," she stuttered, trying to recover. "What's your mother doing that's especially aggravating? Actually," she amended, "don't tell me. I don't want to get involved."

"If you're a true bridesmaid for hire, you should know that mothers of the bride always drive their daughters insane. Or push them into getting sloshed on their wedding day so they can't walk down the aisle without teetering. I'd wager a bet you've seen that up close and personal if you hire yourself out."

Her cousin made her sound like she was a call girl. "That's true," Chloe admitted, thinking of Sarah Schultz's mother out in the Bay Area, who tried to micromanage every aspect of her daughter's wedding. So much that Sarah came *this close* to ordering her mother to stay away from the ceremony.

In an effort to take the pressure off of Sarah and help her have a good wedding day, Chloe concocted outrageous stories about accidentally forgetting Sarah's mother at home —or suggesting that a cousin kidnap her. The only downside was that Sarah laughed so hard she nearly split her side seams while dressing for the wedding rehearsal, but Chloe only had to whip out her sewing kit and mend the crisis.

"Are you the same as a wedding planner?" Mercedes asked, steering the conversation back to her original question.

"Nope, a wedding planner helps rent the church, organizes the caterers, flowers, invitations, and all the reception details. Think of me more as the bride's personal assistant."

"Sorry for all the questions. Can you do anything that the bride wants you to do?"

"In a nutshell—yes," Chloe replied. "You have a dress issue, I can help. You forgot your makeup bag, I can run errands. Your other bridesmaids are flakes, I can whip them into shape. You need help writing a speech for the reception to tell your new husband he's the man of your dreams, I have a degree in creative writing. I can do flowery sentiments or false promises."

Mercedes actually giggled at that, and Chloe stared at the receiver in shock. Her cousin's demeanor was usually prim and proper. She'd make a perfect senator's wife.

"Okay, it only happened once," Chloe admitted with a grin. "A speech filled with false declarations of love, that is."

"The girl actually went through with the wedding? To someone she didn't love?"

"Let's just say the bride had the wedding jitters so bad she almost backed out. But she went through with it and danced until two in the morning."

"Are they separated now?" Mercedes asked, assuming the worst.

"Not at all. They're about to have their first child next month."

"That is simply too peculiar, Chloe. These people—these brides—you work for do not sound ready for marriage."

"Weddings bring out the worst in people." Chloe twirled a pencil between her fingers, a thousand tasks from her to-do list running through her mind. "I know I have an unusual job, but what did you call about? Yes, I can confirm that my family will be in attendance at your wedding next week. Got our e-tickets all ready to go," she added brightly.

"Actually," Mercedes said, "I want to hire you, Chloe."

Chloe took a gulp of her Diet Coke, but the ice had melted, turning the drink watery and warm. "I'm sure you have a dozen best friends that are doing you the honor of being your bridesmaid."

"That's not exactly true," her cousin said slowly. "Since we're getting married at my parents' home instead of a big church or hall, I was only going to have three attendants. And they've all backed out."

Chloe stifled a gasp. Three bridesmaids had canceled on her? That was almost unheard of. "That's terrible. I'm so sorry."

"It's *not* what you're obviously thinking," Mercedes went on coolly.

"I'm—I'm not thinking anything," Chloe assured her.

"My old roommate from college just joined the Peace Corps and left for Africa this morning. Another childhood friend is about to give birth any day, and my younger sister has decided to boycott the wedding."

"That's a drastic measure. Why would Celine not see you married?"

Mercedes gave a dramatic sigh. "We had an argument last night. She hates the idea of spending money on a lavish wedding. She's into the whole concept of minimalism. Lives in a studio apartment in the basement of somebody's house, volunteers at the soup kitchen twice a week, and likes to grow her own vegetables. She even got rid of most of her shoes. She only owns one pair now."

"The horror," Chloe said drily, amusement spreading across her face. "So, Celine has rejected the idea of filthy lucre."

"In a manner of speaking," Mercedes sniffed.

Chloe had worked for enough brides to understand the underlying panic Mercedes was trying to hold at bay. Knowing her cousin, Mercedes was hiding the fact that her pride was hurt by her sister's rejection—although Chloe often had her doubts about a warm heart underneath Mercedes's ice-queen persona.

Her cousin needed a bridesmaid. Any bridesmaid, even one for hire, to save face in front of her guests.

"What are your rates—or is there a family plan? Hint, hint."

"I'm actually in the middle of other jobs. Most brides hire me months out from their wedding date." Chloe flipped through her calendar. Her next on-site wedding wasn't for two more weeks, although she'd lose a few days flying out early for Mercedes. She'd just have to work extra hours when she returned home, but she couldn't resist giving her cousin a hard time. "Hey, I was going to kick back with Granny Zaida and gorge off the buffet table, not stand in a receiving line. Boy, you're asking a lot, blood relative or not."

"Oh, goodness, Chloe, just name your price. Surely, it can't be that much. You'd probably faint at the bill from my wedding planner."

"Define what you want from me. Walk down the aisle in a hideous bridesmaid dress? Chat up lonely guests? Be the first on the dance floor and make a fool of myself? Gather all the single women for the bouquet throw? Run interference between you and your mother? Dance with drunk Uncle Stan?"

"Oh, that all sounds fantastic!"

The relief in Mercedes's voice threw Chloe for a loop. The girl was actually desperate, and a twinge of empathy rose in her throat. Mercedes Romano was one of the D.C. society elite's, and her wedding was probably going to be a major event.

"Hey, we don't have a drunk Uncle Stan!" Mercedes suddenly said.

"Oops, that was my last wedding." She laughed, and Mercedes seemed to relax a little.

"I'd also like you to help me write up something to say for my vows to Mark. I hadn't even thought of that part yet. The list keeps growing!"

"Don't panic, your wedding will be perfect. Okay, my rate for all that is normally fifteen hundred, but you don't have to pay me. We're family, after all."

"We'll discuss that more fully when you get here," Mercedes interrupted. "You don't charge sales tax, do you?"

"We won't talk about filthy lucre any longer and if your wedding is in a week, we need to get going. I need you to send me a bridesmaid dress pronto. You did order brides-maid dresses, correct?"

"Of course. Text me your measurements, and I'll have one of the dresses altered. I have a size 6, 8, and 10. You're not a 12 or a 14 are you?"

Chloe bit her lips to keep the sarcastic retort from

leaking out. "A size 8 will do nicely. With an alteration for length—I'm probably taller than your other friends."

"Oh, you must have lost weight since I saw your family Christmas picture."

Chloe squelched the annoyance rising up her throat. Mercedes could be so passive-aggressive.

"There's just one more thing," Mercedes said. "I have something else to tell you. Something you may not like."

Continue reading THE UNDERCOVER BRIDESMAID here!

FREE on Kindle Unlimited!

SNEAK PEEK: THE NEIGHBOR'S SECRET

BY KIMBERLEY MONTPETIT

It was the perfect day for a wedding. After months of trying on wedding gowns, ordering invitations, and searching every bridal boutique in Toronto for the perfect shoes, Allie Strickland was ready to walk—maybe even run—down the aisle of the church and into Sean Carter's waiting arms.

She'd licked stamps to post the more than one hundred announcements until her tongue was dry. She'd suffered through at least that many long-distance phone calls with her mother that sometimes ended in arguments and tears.

But finally, that very morning, Allie grabbed a big fat red marker and made an X on the calendar.

"Mrs. Sean Carter, here I come," she whispered as she capped the pen and tossed it inside a packing box.

During their five years of dating, she and Sean had gone through grad school together, first jobs, and now Sean was climbing the ladder to become a partner with Learner & Associates law firm.

Tonight she'd be with the man of her dreams forever. No more work interruptions. No more hurried lunches. No more agonizingly long street car rides to get to one another's apartments. Lately, they would just meet somewhere in the middle for a late dinner.

Tomorrow, new renters were moving into her apartment on Bloor Street. When she and Sean returned from their honeymoon to the Bahamas, Allie would unpack the boxes sitting inside Sean's apartment and officially move in.

Allie's stomach jumped as she checked the time on her phone. Her wedding began in ninety minutes and it would take at least half of that just to get through Toronto traffic.

She sent a text to Sean and then took several deep breaths to settle her nerves while she mentally went over her wardrobe packed for fun, sun, and the beach on the way to the Episcopal Church, her brother at the wheel and her mother, sister, and best friend Marla rode in the back.

Three bikinis: red, black, and purple.

Slinky dresses for candlelit dinners.

Five pairs of shoes, including a pair of running shoes.

Lingerie and toiletries.

She couldn't *wait* to get on that plane tomorrow morning and leave work and stress and family behind.

Seven perfect days with Sean. Finally, finally, finally.

"I don't think Toronto has ever looked lovelier," Allie

sighed happily, pressing her nose against the window glass like a kid.

She was excited, anxious, and terrified—and missing Sean. She hadn't seen him in three days due to his working overtime so he'd have a few days off for their honeymoon.

"I promise we'll have a longer honeymoon when I'm finished with this current trial," he'd said last week. "A cruise of the Greek Islands in autumn."

"You know all my dreams," she'd told him, throwing her arms around his neck and feeling the beat of his heart against hers.

Sean had given her a peck goodbye. "You know I have to be in the courtroom at seven a.m., Allie."

She'd frowned, turning away to stare out the window of her apartment. It was a spectacular view of downtown and the lake. She'd been lucky to get this flat a year ago and hated to let it go, but Sean had a bigger place so she'd reluctantly given up her dream apartment.

"That case has taken over your life. *Our* lives," she said, trying not to complain. "We haven't been out in ages. We've hardly kissed in months."

"But we're getting married in a few days, Allie. Be a grown-up and get used to the hectic life of a criminal defense lawyer."

She despised those moments when he treated her like a child. But all she could say was, "But I *miss* you. Don't you miss me?"

As soon as she spoke the words, Allie chomped down on

her tongue. Sentiments like those merely underscored his assessment of her as a petulant child.

"Don't sit on your dress!" Mrs. Strickland suddenly shrieked, motioning to her son that there was a red light.

"These darn no-left-turn streets," Jake muttered, braking so hard they all lunged forward. "They've got the next two streets blocked off for a 10K run."

Quickly, Allie hitched up the beaded satin wedding gown around her to prevent wrinkles on the back end.

"You simply *can't* have wrinkles when you walk down the aisle," her sister Erin said with a dose of sarcasm. "It would be, like, a crime or something."

Mrs. Strickland gave her youngest daughter a second glare and then silently held out her palm when Erin snapped her gum.

Erin stuck her wad of chewing gum in her mother's hand, smashing it down vehemently in revenge, and leaned back with a sulk.

"Thanks for the gum sacrifice," Allie told her, nudging at her sister's shoulder.

"Huh," Erin grunted, sliding another pack of spearmint contraband from her handbag.

"Look at the blue sky and enjoy the fact that there isn't ten feet of snow on the ground."

"You mean smog and obnoxiously tall concrete they call architecture."

"You only think that because you're sixteen."

"Girls!" their mother cried, craning her neck to squint at

the name of the cross street. "Don't fight on your wedding day."

Jake remained stoic, his mobile giving out directions in a British accent.

"It's not *my* wedding day," Erin said, making one of her famous faces, eyes wide, nostrils flaring.

"Obviously. But today is Allie's most special day in her entire life. Be nice. Mind your manners. And *please* don't put your chewed gum on the dinner plate at the reception this evening."

"I'm not eight!" Erin crossed her arms over the deep maroon bridesmaid dress. Lower cut in the bust line than Mrs. Strickland had suggested, but nobody had listened to her protests when the wedding planning rose to extreme levels of tension.

Marla Perry, Allie's best friend since kindergarten, reached over with a tissue. "You've got a smudge of frosting on your face, Allie."

"Where?" Allie scrabbled inside her white lace-covered wedding bag for a mirror, which, of course, only held two tissues and a lipstick for refreshing. Allie had a tendency to bite off her lip color. "How could you let me leave the house like that?"

"It's just a tiny smidge," Marla assured her. "Probably cream cheese from the cinnamon roll."

"You just *had* to go and make your to-die-for cinnamon rolls on the day I wanted to be my skinniest self," Allie teased.

"I knew you'd go all day without food if I didn't give you something. And then we'd be picking you up off the floor in front of the minister when you fainted from starvation."

"Not starvation. Sugar overload. I should have had a granola bar."

"Granola bars are for birds, not real people," Marla said. "Fainting can be a means to an end. Sean can scoop you up from the cold floor and kiss you passionately."

Marla had snagged the lead role in *Romeo and Juliet* in their high school drama production class and swore she'd leave the tiny town of Heartland Cove and run away to New York City. She'd gotten as far as Toronto—which, for a Heartland Cove resident, that boasted a population of 899—was a major feat. But her fine arts degree in photography was proving difficult to find a decent paying job.

"Mom. Chill," Jake said. Miss British GPS voice told him to turn right, but when he did he hit another red light and jerked to a stop. All the women braced a hand on their seats, then adjusted dresses and jewelry.

"Warn us next time, Jake," Mrs. Strickland said, the frown deepening between her eyes.

Allie had not missed the family dynamics living in Toronto, although she sometimes got nostalgic for Heartland Cove, the town where she'd been born, worked her teen summers at the Strickland Family Fry Truck, and had her first kiss on the Bridge of Heartland Cove with a boy who told her he'd love her forever—and then promptly moved to

Newfoundland three weeks later. It might as well have been Timbuktu.

After a few sexy Facebook messages, he'd posted a picture of himself with a suntanned blond girl—and disappeared from her life forever.

In Heartland Cove he'd been her only possibility for a boyfriend until she'd met Sean her senior year as an undergrad in business school.

Sean Carter was the complete opposite of the boy from tiny Heartland Cove High; tall, slim and dark-haired with smoldering eyes and a crooked grin that melted her heart.

"I think butterflies have set up permanent housekeeping in my stomach," Allie said, glancing at the clock ticking down the minutes until she said the words, *I do.*

Mrs. Strickland patted her hand. A little bit comforting. A little bit impatiently. And a little bit sadly.

"You all right Mom?" Allie asked.

Her mother gave a wan smile, and a tug of empathy rose in Allie's chest. She'd never seen her mother wearing red lipstick. Any makeup really. Frying hamburgers and fries for the tourists that swarmed the town every day wasn't exactly conducive to glamour.

Heartland Cove's main industry were the buses that disgorged tourists three times a day to gawk at the Heartland Cove Bridge—North American's longest covered bridge.

Mrs. Strickland brushed off any discomfort she was feeling. "I'm a fish out of water in the glamour of Toronto."

"You look lovely, Mom."

Her mother was wearing a maroon sheath trimmed in lace, black pumps, pantyhose, and a ton of hairspray in a traditional middle-aged pouf. A far cry from jeans and a splattered, greasy apron.

Her cell phone began to buzz, and she recognized the familiar ring of her fiancé. "It's Sean!" she shrieked, patting at her dress and then peering along the floorboard of the car. "I can't find my phone! I talked to him just before we left the apartment. What if he got in an accident?"

"Calm down," Jake said, speeding through a light. He turned to give Allie a grin. "Knowing him, he's calling about the cop giving him a speeding ticket right about now."

"Be useful and help me find my phone, Erin!"

Her sister pressed her lips together and folded her arms across her chest, tapping one toe on the floor mat.

"Okay, sorry," Allie quickly corrected. "I'm sorry. I don't know why I'm panicking."

"Wedding day jitters," Marla said soothingly, searching under the car seats.

Allie lifted wads of satin as delicately as possible. She shook out the folds of her gown, but there was no sign of the phone. It was as if it had disappeared into another dimension.

"I wish you'd gotten married in Heartland Cove, sweetheart," Mrs. Strickland said wistfully.

The ringing had stopped by now and Allie's stomach clenched. Sean had trained her to never miss a phone call from anyone.

He always said that if they were going to excel at their careers and strive for every possible promotion, they could open their own law firm one day, Allie as office manager and head of PR. "Let no opportunity go to waste," Sean said. "Grab them all."

"My phone couldn't have vanished into thin air."

"It's probably on the floor," Erin said with a yawn.

"Can you help me reach down and get it?"

Erin heaved a second deep sigh and dug around the floor, swishing yards of satin and tulle out of her way.

"Careful of my dress!"

"I'm being careful. And . . . it's not here."

"Marla!" Allie said, panic bringing tears to her eyes.

"Don't you dare cry and mess up that makeup job. Here, grab the seat back and lift your bum." Marla ran her fingers along the leather seat under Allie's wedding gown. "Aha!" She held up the cell phone between two fingers and plopped it into Allie's lap.

"You're a lifesaver." Allie quickly checked her voicemail. Sean's deep voice spoke into her ear. "Hey, Allie, I had to run by the office to pick up a new report for this case. Mr. Thompson said I have to read it tonight. The defendant was caught—well, never mind what he was doing. I can't tell you that. But I *will* be at the church. Hitting green lights now, almost to the office."

His voice abruptly stopped and Allie stared at the lifeless phone. It would have been nice to hear an "I love you," but perhaps he'd found a parking space and run inside the office building.

"What's up?" Marla asked.

"Nothing," she lied. "Everything is fine." Inside, she couldn't help fuming. "He might be five minutes late," she added, just to prepare her family.

She hated when they complained about Sean and his awful work schedule. She didn't want to give them any more ammunition than necessary. Sean was there for all the important occasions. Right now was a critical time in his career and when they were able to be together in the same house it would be so much easier to support each other.

"At least your flight isn't until the morning," Erin said, kicking off her tight dress shoes.

"Sean will be there waiting for Allie with the minister," Marla said reassuringly.

Despite her words, the sick feeling grew in Allie's stomach.

In a low voice Marla said, "I know what you're thinking. You don't want to be embarrassed if Sean is late because you know Courtney Willis is going to be in the front row of the church, watching you marry her old boyfriend."

"The front row is reserved for family."

"That was supposed to be a rhetorical statement."

Sadly, Allie knew what she meant. "In what universe is it fair that Sean's old girlfriend gets paired up with *my* fiancé on this new high profile case?"

"In the universe of Ally Strickland," Marla said prophetically.

"That is *not* funny."

"I'm trying to get you to crack a smile. You should be glowing. You're marrying the man of your dreams—not Courtney's dreams. She lost him. Bask in the triumph. Hold your head high."

"Why did Sean invite her in the first place? We had two arguments about Courtney over the past month."

"I stamped all your wedding invitations myself. Sean sent one to every employee at the firm. He couldn't leave her out, especially when they're paired up on this case."

"Why did she RSVP? Didn't she realize it wasn't an event she was expected to actually attend?"

Before Marla could answer, Jake turned off the ignition and jumped out to open the doors all around. "We're here!"

Allie's stomach lurched. The journey to the beautiful little church was over. The moment had arrived.

In less than an hour, she would become Mrs. Sean Carter.

Continue reading THE NEIGHBOR'S SECRET here!

FREE on Kindle Unlimited!

Made in the USA
Columbia, SC
04 October 2024

43590457R00150